CONDEMNED BY SECRETS

A Rolling Brook Novel

Blye Donovan

Condemned by Secrets Copyright © 2022 Blye Donovan

ISBN: 9798986768335
Imprint: Independently published
Cover Design by Central Covers.
Series Logo Design by K.B. Barrett Designs.

DEDICATION

For anyone who has ever seen an abandoned building and imagined what it was and what it could be.

CONTENT WARNING

Contains profanity, mild violence, sexual harassment, and mature sexual content. Also mentions the death of a parent.

CHAPTER 1

Anna

Anna pushed the start button in her brand-new Toyota Camry, then frowned at the display.

What does that funny little symbol mean?

An orange exclamation point taunted her when she didn't have time for problems. Sighing at yet another hiccup in her day, she reached for the glove compartment to retrieve the owner's manual.

Growing up in Washington, D.C., she knew the Washington Metrorail like the back of her hand but the display on her first-ever car—not so much. After a few minutes of searching, she found the symbol.

TPMS. Tire pressure monitor system.

Her frown deepened while she read what it meant, turning her cupid's bow mouth into an attractive pout. Resigned to the fact she'd have to find a gas station with air, Anna turned the car off, then climbed out to inspect her tires.

Fudge! She groaned in frustration when her eyes fell on the back wheel on the driver's side.

It was completely flat.

There was no way she'd make it anywhere driving on *that.*

She closed her eyes and took a calming breath.

You're twenty-four—an adult. You can handle this.

After the pep talk, she opened her eyes and stared at the flat tire. Barely resisting the urge to kick it with one of her shiny nude pumps, she glanced around the Town Hall parking lot, hoping there might be someone who could help her.

The lot was deserted, and even the building looked quiet where it had been bustling with the activity of a town hall meeting a mere hour before. Now, she frowned at the ugly modern structure with its glass siding and minimalist frame. She'd never been a fan of contemporary architecture. It always seemed cold and aloof to her.

Much like the mayor.

Anna's frown deepened as she thought about her conversation with the woman. She glanced around the parking lot one more time, but everyone had cleared out after the meeting while she'd been badgered into agreeing to something she wanted no part in. Rolling her big brown eyes, she grabbed her phone and started to search for how to change a tire.

After ten minutes of how-to videos, she was overwhelmed. Did she even have a lug wrench or a jack? Opening her trunk, she lifted the fabric covering to find out. At least she had a spare and what looked like the scissor jack she'd seen in one of the videos.

She lifted the jack out first and grunted at its unexpected weight. When it came to muscles, she didn't have any. She'd often been called petite, which was a polite way of saying what she knew to be true—she was short and skinny. As a teenager, she'd longed for curves, but her wish, like so many others, had never been granted. Struggling with the jack, she managed to set it on the ground beside her now useless tire.

About to brush back the strands of long brunette hair that had fallen into her face, Anna caught sight of her grease-covered hand and released a sound of disgust.

Why is everything greasy if it's brand new?

It was a good thing she hadn't worn her white blazer today. She'd thought about it in this heat. It was early summer, and the afternoon sun packed quite a punch, but she'd opted for her navy jacket with the matching trousers to look more professional. The town hall meeting had been her introduction to the people of Rolling Brook, and she'd wanted to make a good first impression.

Not that they'd cared.

Thinking about her less-than-stellar reception at the meeting, Anna blinked back tears. She'd agreed to attend under the guise of being presented as the town's new historic preservationist, but she'd been wholly unprepared for what she'd walked into. There seemed to have been two camps of people. Those who wanted to raze all the historic buildings and start fresh, and those who wanted to restore them to their appropriate historical periods and turn them into museums. Neither of which were her plans for Rolling

Brook.

She wanted to rehabilitate the existing historic buildings into new homes and businesses—make them "work" for the town.

But that idea had been met with grumbles and hard stares, so she wasn't sure where that left her. And then the mayor. *Ugh!*

A tear slipped out as she stared down at her filthy fingers. She had nothing to wipe them on; she was as unprepared for her current situation as she was for her new job. Realizing she was wallowing in self-pity, she shook herself and went to retrieve the spare tire.

She'd get through this if she just focused on the task at hand. Though she was young, the challenges she'd faced growing up as the daughter of a high-profile politician in the nation's capital taught her you could only solve one problem at a time, and right now, her most immediate problem was this stupid flat tire.

After lifting out the spare, she leaned it against the bumper and sighed in relief at the sight of the lug wrench stowed beneath. It looked like she had everything she needed to change the flat.

Stepping back from the trunk, she wiped her forehead with the back of her arm and winced when it came away, covered in makeup. She wasn't used to wearing any, but she'd put it on today, knowing it would make her look older. Now, she'd have to get the jacket dry-cleaned. Resigned, she took her blazer off and felt a little bit of relief. The heat beat down on her, making tiny beads of sweat crawl down her back. She thought about rolling up the sleeves of her white shirt, but the dark spots on her fingers made her decide otherwise. She would just be extra careful not to get anything on it. Grabbing the wrench, she bent down to the wheel and placed it over one of the lug nuts just like she'd seen the man do in the video.

Grunting with the effort of a tennis pro smashing the ball, she attempted to turn the wrench, but it didn't budge. She huffed out a breath and slid her rectangle tortoiseshell glasses back up her nose with a knuckle, careful not to get grease on her face. Deciding she'd come back to that lug nut, she moved on to the next one and was met with the same result. She got frustrated, tried all five, and couldn't make any the tiniest bit looser.

How did they come off so easily for the man in the video?

She had to be doing something wrong. Standing up, she held the wrench loosely in her right hand as she studied the tire. What was she missing?

"Excuse me, miss?"

Anna jumped, letting out a shriek as she spun around. She'd been so absorbed she hadn't heard anyone approach. What she saw had her lowering the lug wrench she'd clutched to her chest in defense.

Oh. My. Gravy. Who was this Adonis?

Standing before her was a breathtaking policeman. His hair was caught somewhere between brunette and blonde, the sun making the strands on top a lighter color. It fell over the middle of his forehead in a tousled "V," drawing attention to his pale blue eyes. She'd never seen anything like them before. They were so light they appeared silver as the sun reflected in them. He had a little bit of scruff on his chin as if he'd missed shaving it, and, for some reason, she found that utterly sexy, especially when it contrasted with the smooth line of his perfect nose and square jawline.

"Do you need some help?"

Gawd. Even his voice was sexy. The husky tone wrapped around her like a warm towel, trapping the heat building within her. It was comforting but steamy—much too steamy in this weather. Fresh perspiration broke out on her neck, and she wished she'd pulled her hair up.

He smiled at her, making a dimple appear on his left cheek. Okay, that was just unfair. Not only was he tall and handsome, but he had dimples.

If she'd been awestruck before, now she was nearly frozen. She'd never been good at talking to hot guys. And this cop was uber-hot, like *Magic Mike* hot.

Since she couldn't find her voice to answer him, she nodded, hypnotized by the way the sun glinted off the natural highlights in his hair. They were like strings of gold, and with the silver eyes, he looked too good to be real.

He extended a hand to her and said, "Luther. Are you just passing through? I haven't seen you in town before, and you're—" He looked her up and down, and her cheeks heated.

Was that interest in his eyes? *Impossible.*

"—not someone I'd forget."

She extended her hand in response but jerked it back at the last minute when she remembered her smudged fingers.

The hottie cop raised an eyebrow at her sharp movement, and she winced, holding up her hand for him to see.

"Sorry! I'm Anna."

He chuckled at her hand and pointed at her shirt. "It's already spread."

Confused, she glanced down and cringed. There was a definitive "X" across her chest where the grease had marked it when she'd clutched the lug wrench. No wonder his eyes had raked over her like that.

"Fudgesicles," she grumbled under her breath.

Anna was mortified. Her cheeks were on fire, and she wished she could melt into a puddle and slink away. Why did embarrassing stuff always happen to her? She was cursed. Had to be.

"Did you just say 'fudgesicles'?" His voice startled her; he sounded much closer than he had a moment before.

With a flaming face, she mustered her courage and lifted her head to look at him. He'd moved and stood near enough to touch.

Luther grinned at her, and not only did the dimple in his left cheek reappear, but a matching one flashed at her from his right, making her catch her breath.

No one should be that handsome. There should be a law against it.

At the thought, a nervous giggle bubbled up her throat. She tried to stop it, but it escaped, coming out in the most mortifying of snorts that had her clamping a hand over her mouth.

"Uh-oh." His expression laughed at her.

Her eyes bugged out when he reached for the hand covering her mouth. With his palm closed over hers, she sucked in a breath. His touch sent her overstimulated system into overdrive. The heat simmering inside her spread like wildfire from her inflamed face, searing through the rest of her body.

He pulled her hand away from her mouth, his lips twitching as though he held in a laugh. "You, um"—he cleared his throat around a chuckle and waved a finger at her lips—"got it on your face now."

She groaned and closed her eyes, wishing for the ability to disappear. Right now, she'd trade anything for that superpower or for a do-over. If she could just have one of those—

Wait, why is he still holding my hand?

She opened her eyes at the same time Luther burst out laughing. Frowning at him, she jerked her hand out of his grip.

This is why she preferred being invisible. People didn't notice you enough to laugh at you when you flew under the radar.

Hiding her hurt behind anger, she bit out, "Well, I'm glad one of us is amused."

"Sorry," he managed between chuckles as she stood staring at him, trying to disguise the pain his amusement inflicted. "I just—" More chuckles.

Murphy's law had caught up with her, and now this cop was adding insult to injury by laughing about it.

He cleared his throat and finally stopped. Though his lips had stilled, his eyes shone with mirth. "Why don't you let me take that." He gestured at the lug wrench she still held.

She wasn't a violent person or even a hot-headed one, but she gripped the wrench tighter as she imagined hurling it at his perfect head. Blinking away the fantasy, she handed him the tool, then crossed her arms over her chest.

"Let's get this tire changed out for you." He was smiling, but his eyes had sobered.

"Thanks." *It's the least you can do after laughing at me like that.*

* * * *

Luther

Luther was having trouble concentrating on the simple task in front of him. Anna stood a couple of feet away as he worked on the tire, and he smelled her perfume. It was sweet and fruity, reminding him of Skittles. He loved the brightly colored candies. His fellow officers liked to tease him about it, but he always kept a bag of them in his glove box.

If he hadn't already developed a craving for the tiny brunette, her scent would have done it.

Wait, what?

He shook his head as if the motion would shake away that thought. How could he already want the woman when he'd just met her? He glanced at her out of the corner of his eye.

She leaned against the car, fanning herself with a hand as she stared off into the distance. Her mouth was pursed in thought and made the rosy color of her lips stand out. They looked as good as a ripe strawberry, and he wondered if they'd taste as sweet.

She caught him staring, and her cheeks flushed an attractive shade of pink. He grinned, then turned his attention back to the tire.

"So, what brings you to Rolling Brook?" he asked as he struggled with the last lug nut.

It was clear to him the car was new, and the tire had never been changed. The nuts were still on factory tight. He'd already worked up a sweat loosening the first few.

"I just moved here."

Well, isn't that interesting?

He grinned at the idea of seeing her again as he moved the jack into position. "Welcome to town. Do you need any recommendations on where to stay or eat?" Luther turned to look at her as he cranked the jack.

She stared at him with guarded eyes.

Did I say something to offend her?

Curious, he lifted an eyebrow as he waited for her response.

"No. I mean, thank you, but I'm staying at the bed and breakfast until I find an apartment."

"We'll probably see more of each other then." He turned his attention to the car as he finished cranking the jack. With her vehicle lifted, he started to remove the loosened lug nuts.

"What do you mean?" Her voice was sharp, and when Luther looked up, she'd propped her hands on her hips.

He figured he'd better not point out she was getting more grease on her white shirt, even though he enjoyed getting a rise out of her. Maybe it was the way her face flushed beautifully in anger or the way she managed to look haughtily down her nose at him despite her current disheveled state, but the image had excitement flooding his veins and heating his blood. She was different than any woman he'd ever met.

There was something refined and even a little uptight about Anna. He wondered what it would take to loosen her up. She seemed as stubborn as the lug nuts he'd struggled with, but the challenge only made her more appealing.

Not wanting to scare her off before he had a chance to find out, he gave her an affable smile and went back to the flat. "My mother runs it. I go by every Sunday."

"Oh." He heard her soft reply as he removed the tire from the wheel well.

Checking if it could be patched, he gave it a roll to see what caused the air to leak out. He frowned when he finished the inspection. He'd expected to find a nail or some other sharp object still embedded in the tire, but it was clear this was no accident. The tire had a gash in between the grooves that could only be made by a knife. He'd almost missed it. Whoever had done this had been careful to strike where the cut wouldn't be noticeable.

But who would want to slash the woman's tire? She'd just arrived. Had she already made enemies?

Luther propped the flat against the car and pulled out his phone to take photos. He was going to have to report this.

"What are you doing?" Her tone hinted at her confusion as she watched him take pictures of the puncture.

He straightened and turned to look at her. "Do you have

any idea who would want to slash your tire?"

"What?" Her eyes widened when she realized what he was saying. "Someone cut it?"

He kept his eyes trained on her face as she processed that. The shock gave way to curiosity, and she bent down to get a closer look at the tire. "I've never seen a slashed tire before."

"Anna," he waited for her to look at him.

When she did, her golden-brown eyes had narrowed. "It's just a little cut. How do you know someone did that? Couldn't I have just driven over something sharp?"

"Not likely. The puncture's too perfect." He didn't want to freak her out, but denial wouldn't help him discover who did this.

She frowned at his words, and he tried not to notice how enticing her mouth looked, bowing into a cute little pout that puffed out those full strawberry-colored lips.

Concentrate, Luther!

He cleared his throat and tried again. "Do you know who would want to sabotage your tire?"

She sighed, and her eyes flashed their frustration when she answered, "Honestly? Any number of people who were at the meeting." She shook her head. "Let's just say I didn't make any friends today."

Luther blinked. "Oh. That's right. There was a town hall to introduce the new preservationist, but wait; you're her?" He couldn't help the surprise coloring his voice. "I thought you'd be a little old lady."

He'd smiled to soften the remark, but she still glared at him. "Thanks."

"So, historic preservation, huh? How'd you get into that?" He was genuinely curious. He wanted to know everything about her—where she was from, why she'd studied preservation, whether she had a boyfriend . . .

"Look, Luther. I'm sorry, but I'm already behind schedule. Can you please just change the tire?"

He smiled, undeterred. Her reticence made him want to find out even more. "Sure."

He picked up the spare and finished changing out her tire. As he worked, he told her, "I'll get a list of everyone at the meeting, and there should be camera footage from the building's security system."

With the tire changed, he stood and brushed his hands on his black uniform pants. Then he reached into his pocket for the small notepad he kept there. "I have to file a report on this. I need you to give me your full name and a way to contact you."

She nodded and rattled off her name and phone number. "You already know where I'm staying."

He looked up from his notepad to find her smirking at him. Damned, if that wasn't sexy. He liked her sarcastic streak.

"That I do." He winked and chuckled under his breath as it wiped the smirk off her face.

Two could play this game.

"Right, well. Thank you."

"You're welcome, Anna Hendricks." He liked the sound of her full name. It fit her, just a little haughty but hinting at fun.

With a brusque nod, she climbed into her car. He

waved, then stood grinning as she drove away. He'd been sure his day would be dull.

Rolling Brook had been quiet for the last couple of years. They were barely an hour outside Chicago, but it felt like hundreds of miles. He'd been growing restless in his job and in the town, but he had a feeling that was about to change.

CHAPTER 2

Anna

Anna refused to look in her mirrors as she drove away. She didn't need another glimpse of Officer Eye Candy. Because that's all he was—something nice to look at. She didn't date guys like Luther—jocks who thought they ruled the world. Having been burned by his type before, she'd learned to steer clear.

Sure, he'd helped her, but she had no qualms he would want something in return. And he wasn't going to get it.

No. Way. She was not about to be another name in his little black book, even if he smelled so dang good.

Glancing at the gym towel he'd given her, which was lying in her passenger seat, she remembered the tempting scents of citrus and another earthier one like fresh-cut grass that had met her nose when she'd used it to wipe the grease off her face and hands. Something about that smell had made her want to breathe in deeply.

She hadn't, of course. She'd already embarrassed

herself enough, and no matter how kind he'd been to offer her the towel, she couldn't help wondering what his ulterior motive was.

At the sound of a car horn, Anna jumped and jerked the wheel. She'd been completely lost in thought. Blinking to clear her head, she corrected the vehicle just in time to keep it from running over the curb.

Get it together, Anna!

She needed to snap out of it before she arrived at the office of the Rolling Brook Historical Preservation Society. It was already fifteen minutes past the time she'd told the society she'd be there. With the mayor holding her up and then the flat, her day had veered *way* off course.

She wasn't convinced someone had slashed her tire, but she wasn't overly worried about it if they had. It was merely a hazing ritual, a "not-so-welcome" welcome to the town. She knew she was the outsider here, and many thought her city background meant she had no idea what this small town needed. But she was determined to prove them wrong. This was her first real job, and she had to succeed at it if she had any hope of moving on to bigger and better things.

To accomplish that, she had to correct the course her day was on, which meant making sure this next meeting went better than the last one. She drummed her fingers against the wheel as she thought about what the mayor had told her.

Mayor Landstrom was clearly in the camp of people who felt Rolling Brook could use some modernizing. The woman had practically conveyed to Anna her job might not be funded much longer.

Her hands tightened on the steering wheel as she recalled the mayor's attitude. Oh, the woman had been polite, sure, but also condescending. Then she'd forced Anna to agree to be on the Development Review Committee because they needed a representative from a cultural organization.

While reviewing plans for development within the town to ensure they met with the town's policies wasn't entirely at odds with her job description, being on the committee irked her because the mayor had remarked it would be her way of providing value to the town.

As if she couldn't do that in other ways! *Ugh!*

It had been insulting. Anna wasn't sure whether that was the mayor's intention. The woman was hard to read, but then politicians usually were.

As the daughter of one, she'd met several who'd become so used to pretending that their plastic smiles were permanently plastered on their faces.

It doesn't matter.

She shook off the bad memories. She would just stay out of the mayor's way as much as possible because she didn't need enemies, powerful or otherwise.

The rehabilitated building made her smile as she pulled into a parking spot in front of the historical preservation office. It was a three-story Federal-style house glowing with a cheerful shade of blue-green paint. The gray brick of the lower level was an eloquent contrast to the colored clapboard siding. This was what she wanted for Rolling Brook. More vibrant historical structures supporting the modern uses the town needed. She'd done her homework and knew both office and living space were in high demand for the small downtown area, which is why her mission was to save more historic buildings by adding to the supply.

With a brighter mood, Anna reached for her leather tote and caught sight of the clock in her dash.

Oh Snap! She was now twenty minutes late.

As someone who was habitually early, the tardiness bothered her. Frustration tightened the band around her head, threatening to erupt into a full-on migraine. The state of her clothes compounded it. She hadn't had time to go back to the bed and breakfast and change, so she would just have to wear her blazer buttoned all the way up and hope no one saw the dark streaks of grease on her shirt.

Grumbling under her breath, she hurried to the building. Like many of the era, this 1820s structure had a full-height basement level, but the main entrance was on the second floor. Halfway up the side-facing stairs, her skinny heels slipped on the uneven stone, and she had to grab onto the iron railing to stop herself from falling. Huffing out a forceful breath that moved the hair out of her eyes, Anna righted herself and climbed the last few steps with more caution.

Before she managed to reach the door, it flew open. "Oh, dear! All you all right, hon? We saw you slip, and Dorothy thought for sure you were a goner. I'm so glad you didn't fall. We always use the back entry because those stairs can be tricky. Here, let me take that for you."

Her eyebrows squished together as she stared at the chatty brunette who grabbed the bag off her shoulder. The woman had thrown the string of sentences at her so fast that she wasn't sure which one to respond to.

The talkative brunette looked to be in her fifties. She sported a few wrinkles on her carefully made-up face, but the deep blue hue of her eyes struck Anna. They shone with excitement as she gestured for her to come inside.

She entered the building and followed the woman into what had once been the parlor. It now served as a reception area, but not much had changed apart from the addition of two desks facing each other. The room had beautiful, restored hardwood floors and reproduction floral wallpaper.

"I'm Sandy." The brunette turned and pointed at a white-haired older woman seated behind one of the desks. "This is Dorothy. Rosie had to leave, but you can meet her tomorrow. Then there's Richard—"

"Oh, he's such a nice boy!" Dorothy chimed in while Anna's head was ready to explode.

She needed a moment to catch her breath, but it didn't seem like she would get one. "Sandy?"

"Yes?" The one-word answer was almost a surprise after the rate the woman had just been going.

Anna took a deep breath and rubbed at the headache in her temple. "Thank you for the rundown, but aren't we all meeting together? I know I'm a few minutes behind schedule, and I apologize for that." She sighed. "I had a flat tire after the town hall and—"

"Oh! How did that go? I can't wait to hear all about it. Did you meet the mayor then? She's a handful, that one. Well, we'll tell you about her later, hon. First, let's get you settled. Come, I'll show you to your office."

When Sandy grabbed her hand, Anna gave in and let the older woman usher her down the hall. They passed the dining room, which had been converted into a conference area, a small, updated bathroom, and another office before she found herself staring at a closed door with a plaque that read, 'Anna Hendricks, Director.'

Tears welled in her eyes at the sight. She was as honored as she was anxious, staring at that title. She'd never been a director of anything, and its weight was already heavy on her shoulders.

"Here we are!" Sandy announced with a huge smile. When her eyes met Anna's, the older woman patted her hand gently. "There, now. You've had a day. I can tell. Why don't I give you a few minutes to get settled, and then you find us when you're ready?"

"Thank you." Anna nodded and took her tote back from Sandy, who retreated down the hall.

Grateful for the time to herself, she grasped the antique brass knob and turned. Her breath caught at the beauty of her new office.

It's like a museum!

Gorgeous antique furniture surrounded her. She moved to sit behind the writing desk hewn from tiger maple and ran her hands over the smooth, polished wood. As she caressed the desk, a smile bloomed on her face. She felt like a kid at Christmas.

Hopping up, she walked to the opposite side of the room and admired the ornate floor-to-ceiling bookcases covering the wall. They were a darker maple than the desk and sported carved pilasters that she instantly fell in love with. The faux columns gave the bookcases such a regal air.

They were filled with books on different types of architecture and conservation technologies. She ran her fingers along the spines and noted she owned most of them from her studies. But there were a few she didn't have and would love to delve into. The more resources she had, the better because the more knowledge at her disposal, the less likely she was to mess anything up.

Saving historic structures could be tricky, but she was a champion researcher. It was her favorite pastime, and she had gotten very good at it in college. It didn't matter that her classmates had teased her for being all work and no play. To her, finding a hidden piece of history was more fun than getting drunk and puking your guts out.

Shaking off the melancholy those thoughts brought on, Anna grabbed a book on the history of Rolling Brook and carried it to her desk. She reached for her bag and pulled out her laptop. When she opened it, she noticed how dim the office was. There was an overhead lamp, but she preferred natural light.

She stepped to the window to open the ornate damask curtains. They were a deep shade of burgundy and matched well with the flowery wallpaper. Still, they were so heavy they acted as room-darkening drapes.

Struggling to push them aside, she finally succeeded and grinned at the historic six-over-six window before her. It had the original wooden sash and wavy glass panes. It glinted as the sun shone in, brightening her mood and the room. The preservation society had done well in rehabilitating this place. It excited her to see what else they'd been able to do.

Grabbing her portfolio and fountain pen out of her bag, she was in a much calmer frame of mind than when she'd first arrived. After one last glance around her office, she backed into the hall and ran smack into a wall.

"Oof!" She couldn't help the exclamation before she spun around.

"Sorry!" a man's voice said at the same time.

Her gaze tracked up the Hugo-boss-covered wall. His suit was sharp, but his face was friendly. He had a charming smile and pleasant brown eyes, which matched his wavy dark hair.

"You're Anna." The wall stretched out his hand. "I'm Richard. I consult for the society on outreach programs."

She clasped his hand, then frowned down at it when he squeezed hers a little too tight. Shaking her fingers loose, she said, "Yes, nice to meet you. I was coming to ask everyone to join me in the conference room."

"I saw you at the town hall meeting." His smile stayed welcoming, but she thought his eyes narrowed at her for a second.

Noting their amiable look now, she dismissed the thought. "Oh? What did you think of it?"

He chuckled. "I think you got a dose of what the rest of us have been dealing with."

"Ah. Well, I guess I'm glad it's not just me. At least we're all in this battle together." She smiled and thought she saw that flash of anger again in his gaze.

"That we are. Shall we?" He gestured for her to go first.

"After you."

She hesitated. Something about the way he'd said it made her scalp prickle with unease. She stared at Richard, but his expression was the same genial one he'd been wearing before.

Brushing it off, she turned and started down the hallway. It was time to meet the rest of her team and get to work.

* * * *

Luther

Luther whistled as he walked into the police station. Running into Anna had significantly improved his mood. He'd gone from being frustrated at responding to another pointless dispute between neighbors to being excited about his job again. Not only that, but he was plenty interested in the new girl in town.

Ignoring his fellow officers' stares and raised eyebrows, he breezed through the bullpen to his desk. When he reached it, he smirked at the mountain of loose Skittles covering it. The desks were arranged in groups of four, and he figured either Peterson or Haines, who sat closest to him, had thought he deserved some ribbing.

"Thanks for the snack," he called out to whoever had left them.

He sat down and brushed the candies off his keyboard before grabbing a handful and popping them into his mouth. The fruity flavors exploded on his taste buds as he chewed, and his thoughts returned to Anna.

She'd smelled like Skittles. Would she taste like them, too?

He was dying to find out if her strawberry lips were sweet or tart. Either was appealing, as was the caramel of her eyes. He'd been struck by their color, even hidden behind those cute glasses. Not quite brown, they teetered on gold, and against her pale skin, the contrast made quite the picture. A picture he was looking forward to seeing again. Thankfully, he had a reason too. Maybe she'd even—

"Hey!" Luther flinched when a folder hit him in the head.

He turned to find Sergeant Jameson hovering over him. His superior's arms were crossed, and his blue eyes squinted down at Luther. A lock of red hair had fallen over the sergeant's forehead, but it did nothing to detract from the toughness his stature promised.

"I called your name five times, Monroe."

Luther grinned, unable to stop thoughts of Anna from flooding in. "Sorry."

The sergeant handed him the folder he'd hit him with.

"What's this, Sarge?"

Luther opened it, but before he had a chance to flip through, Sergeant Jameson spoke, "I'll tell you what it's not. The report you owe me on that hit and run last week."

Luther rubbed at the back of his neck and shrugged. "Because that wasn't a hit and run. Not really. How am I supposed to write up a speeding car hit a cow and fled the scene?"

"Sounds like you just did. Type it up, Monroe. I want it on my desk before the end of your shift."

"Done." He smiled, and Sergeant Jameson raised an

eyebrow.

"Why are you suddenly so happy? You've been moping around for weeks."

"Stopped on a call on my way in. We've got a tire slasher." He couldn't keep the smile out of his voice.

"And that's a reason to smile because . . .?"

"Because I'm going to find out who did it."

Sergeant Jameson's eyes narrowed at Luther as if he knew there was more to the story. "And?"

"And I get to follow up with Miss Anna Hendricks, who will be so impressed she'll agree to go out with me."

Sarge shook his head at Luther and barked out a laugh. "Leave it to you to make this about a woman. So, she's the victim?"

"Yep. Just moved here. She's the historical society's new preservationist." He grabbed another handful of Skittles and tossed them in his mouth. At the sergeant's glare, Luther offered him some. "Ski-ls?" he mumbled as he chewed.

With a sharp shake of his head, Sergeant Jameson inquired, "Does she want to press charges?"

He swallowed and frowned. He hadn't asked her that—specifically. "Not sure. Does it matter?"

The sergeant sighed and ran a hand down his face. "Yes. Come on, Monroe. That's a rookie mistake. Did you get so distracted you forgot how to do your job?"

Luther's neck heated at the comment, and he sat straighter in his chair. He respected the hell out of Sergeant Jameson. The man had been on the force long enough to make Lieutenant, but Captain Grouse was causing a backlog on the promotion front.

He didn't like disappointing Sarge. Maybe he had been a little too distracted by Anna.

Clearing his throat, he attempted to redeem himself. "I've got her contact, I'll get in touch and find out, but I wanted to have something to lead with first. I've already got the list of attendees from the town hall meeting where her tire was damaged. I'm going after the security footage from the parking lot next. They use a third-party agency, so all the data is stored off-site."

"I figured, but if you want the captain to sign off on the request, he's not going to be interested unless this woman's pressing charges. He won't tangle with the mayor if he doesn't have to." Sergeant Jameson's eyes cut to Captain Grouse's office door, and he frowned.

Neither of them was fond of the captain, and Luther knew the man liked to make things difficult. But he wasn't sure what Sarge meant about the mayor. "What does the mayor have to do with it? I just need to speak with the security company."

The sergeant's eyes sparked at the question. "She monitors everything that goes on in that building. She'll shut you down fast if you don't run it by her first."

Luther sighed, then nodded. "10-4, Sarge."

The sergeant's face broke out in a grin, and he clasped Luther on the shoulder. "Good luck."

He started to walk away when Luther stopped him. "Wait, what about this?" He held up the folder Sarge had assaulted him with.

Sergeant Jameson shook his head. "Give it to Haines.

You're going to have bigger fish to fry."

He frowned after the sergeant. Would the mayor really be a problem? You'd think she'd want to know if someone was slashing tires in her parking lot.

Luther scratched his head with frustrated fingers and left several blonde strands sticking up at odd angles.

Great. Now I've got two women to charm.

CHAPTER 3

Luther

The next day, Luther found himself on a call that was an exercise in frustration. He sat hunched over, his elbows leaning on his desk, as he pinched the bridge of his nose and hoped the headache developing between his eyes didn't spread.

Hanging up the phone, he sighed. The noise of the bullpen echoed around him. Phones rang, and officers yelled, but he was used to tuning all that out. His thoughts focused on the fact he'd gotten nowhere with the mayor's office. The best they were able to do was make him an appointment with the woman for the end of next week.

He straightened and stared blankly at his computer screen; his thoughts stuttered as though they'd come up against a brick wall. If this had been a different crime, he'd have pushed the cop card and demanded to see the mayor sooner. But with no one hurt and him not even sure the victim wanted to press charges, he had little ground to stand on.

No use pissing the woman off.

He shook his head to clear it. Everyone knew the mayor liked being in a position of authority. She was the type of woman who enjoyed lording power over others. He needed her cooperation, and he'd never see the security footage if he challenged her.

The document on his computer screen swam before his tired eyes. He blinked a few times to bring it into focus. At least he'd made *some* progress. He was halfway through the names of people who'd attended the meeting at Town Hall when Anna's tire had been slashed. He'd spent the morning working his way down the list while waiting for the mayor's office to call him back. Over thirty attended, and so far, no one had noticed the flat tire or anything suspicious.

He ran a hand down his face in frustration and frowned when his stomach growled. He glanced at his watch.

2:34 p.m.

Realizing he'd missed lunch, Luther thought maybe it was time for a break. He needed to follow up with the victim anyway. Find out if she wanted to press charges or not. He could've called her this morning to ask, but he'd wanted to put the question to her in person. His eyes gleamed, and the corner of his mouth tipped up.

He was happy to use any excuse to see her again. He wondered what she'd be wearing today and if he could fluster her and spread that enticing blush across her cheeks. Smiling at the prospect, Luther pushed back his chair and rose.

As soon as his head cleared the partitions, Sergeant Jameson called his name, "Monroe!"

He winced, annoyed that his plan to leave would be delayed, and turned around. "Sarge?"

"Got something for you. Come take a look." The sergeant beckoned with his baseball mitt of a hand as his eyes stayed trained on his computer screen.

When Luther reached Sergeant Jameson's desk, he leaned down to look over the man's broad shoulders, and his eyes widened at what was on the screen. It was a sonogram. "Congratulations!" He clasped the sergeant on the shoulder.

Sergeant Jameson jumped at the contact, shrugging Luther's hand off in the process, and closed the sonogram picture. "Shit! That's not what I wanted you to look at. Here." He turned and shoved a folder at Luther. "Stop hovering over me and tell me what you think."

Luther took the folder but couldn't help the silly grin that crossed his face. This would be the sergeant's first kid. "Boy or girl?"

Sergeant Jameson shook his head. "I don't know. This was the first ultrasound. Look, Monroe," his voice sharpened, and he speared Luther with a look that brooked no room for argument. "You weren't supposed to see that. It's too early to tell people, all right? You can't say anything, or Daisy'll have my balls."

He chuckled, knowing the sergeant's wife could be a real ball-buster, but as he took notice of the man's glare, Luther sobered and mimed, zipping his lips closed.

He opened the folder Sergeant Jameson had given him

and scanned the report. As he read, his eyebrows knitted, and his mouth firmed into a thin line.

Having finished it, he glanced back up at the sergeant. "Is there anything to this?"

Sergeant Jameson crossed his arms and leaned back in his chair. "You tell me. Haines was skeptical, which is why I want your eyes on it. I'm not dismissing something like this. Not if it has even the slightest possibility of being legit."

Luther nodded, stunned by what he'd just read. Possibilities swarmed in his head. As the shock wore off, excitement flooded in, and his blood raced along with his thoughts. "I'm on it, Sarge."

"Good."

He strode away, dropping the folder on his desk on his way out of the building. He was still planning to talk to Anna, but now, he had another stop to make.

* * * *

Luther

At the outskirts of town stood a brand new strip mall—The Shoppes at Rolling Brook. It was completed six months ago, and businesses were slowly filling in. So far, there was a pizza shop, a cash advance place, a knick-knack store, a hair salon, and a small grocer's market. The developer was out of Chicago and modeled the shopping center after the city's Southport Corridor.

Even though the buildings along the strip were new construction, they were a mix of historic and modern architectural styles, making them look like they fit with Rolling Brook's aesthetic. The problem was it was built to look like a street lined with shops when it sat in the middle of nowhere. It looked out of place amidst the surrounding hills and farmland, almost like a ghost town.

A few storefronts remained vacant, but the mayor was confident they'd be occupied before the year was up. At least that's what she said anytime someone brought it up at a town hall meeting. Luther wasn't sure if she knew something the town wasn't privy to or if it was her attempt at placating them.

Mulling that over, he pulled into the parking lot in front of the row of stores. It held only a handful of cars, which suited him just fine. He needed to have a conversation with a worker at Lou's Pizzeria, and the less chance of being overheard, the better.

But the lack of activity didn't go unnoticed. Either this place was losing money, or something else was going on. Judging by the file he'd just read, he was betting on the latter. And he was going to find out, starting by talking to the person who'd triggered the Suspicious Activity Report.

* * * *

Luther

Luther pushed his conversation with the informant from the pizza shop to the back of his mind as he made his way to the back door of the preservation society's office. The guy had given him a lot to think about, but he wanted to let it simmer on the back burner before he made any drastic moves. Tipping his hand too soon was a surefire way to end the investigation before it began.

And he had another investigation to take care of at the moment, like finding out as much as he could about Anna Hendricks.

He couldn't help the grin of anticipation that lit his face as he opened the back door to the building. It opened into the society's gift shop, which offered books on local history, hand-crafted jewelry, and reproductions of Native American artifacts. Ware littered the shelves and the central table, but the room was empty of people.

He wandered past the cash register into the hallway. Poking his head in the rest of the rooms on the ground floor, he found them similarly empty. This part of the building was set up as a museum. It included vignettes of life in the house from different periods of history. He knew the society did tours a couple of days a week, but today didn't look like one of them.

He began climbing the stairs to the second floor and flinched when they creaked under his weight. The house was so quiet the sound echoed off the walls. He didn't put much stock in the supernatural, but if ghosts were real, he could believe they lived in old houses like this one.

The hairs on the back of his neck stood up at the thought, and he laughed softly at himself. If anyone was here, ghosts or otherwise, he'd just sent up a flare with that noise.

A man appeared at the top of the stairs as if to prove him right. He was tall and slim-looking in his tailored suit. Judging by the few grays at his temples, Luther thought the man was probably a couple of years older than his twenty-nine years. The rest of his hair was brown, as were his eyes, and he stared down at Luther with a confused expression on his face.

"Can I help you, officer?"

Luther smiled. "I hope so."

The man didn't respond, but his posture was stiff as he stepped back, waiting for him to climb the rest of the stairs.

"I'm looking for Anna Hendricks," he told him when he'd reached the landing.

The man visibly relaxed and answered, "I'm afraid you've just missed her. She's gone out to tour our properties with Ms. Rosie."

Luther shrugged, undeterred. He'd come back or . . . even better, he'd drop by the bed and breakfast. A home-cooked meal sounded like a good idea, and he knew his mom would be happy to have him over for dinner. "Bad timing on my part. Thanks, Mr. . . . .?"

"Richard Cartwright."

Guess my trip's not wasted after all.

He recognized the name from his list of attendees at the town hall but gave no outward indication of that fact. Instead, he kept his smile easy as he addressed Cartwright, "Mind if I ask you a few questions?"

Cartwright blinked at him, the confusion evident on his face. "What about?"

"Were you aware Miss Hendricks's car was vandalized yesterday?"

Cartwright's eyes widened. "No. When did this happen?"

Sizing the man up, Luther noted his surprise seemed

genuine, so he continued with his line of questioning. "After the town hall meeting. I understand you attended?"

Cartwright nodded.

"Did you see anyone loitering around Miss Hendricks's vehicle?"

"No, I don't even know what she drives." Cartwright smiled and shrugged. "I just met her yesterday."

He sighed inwardly. This was another non-starter. "What about anything that struck you as suspicious?"

Cartwright shook his head. "Nothing I can think of, but I left right after the meeting."

"Okay, well, if you think of anything, give me a call."

"Sure, officer."

"Thanks. I'll see myself out."

Luther turned and started down the stairs. He paused when he thought he heard a whispered "good luck," but on glancing back up, Cartwright was gone.

Shaking off the feeling of being taunted, he descended the stairs. He wasn't sure what, but something about Cartwright had his Spidey senses tingling.

* * * *

Anna

At the last minute, Rosie directed Anna to turn left. She slammed on the brakes, eliciting a honk from the car behind them and a sharp gasp from Rosie.

"Sorry!" She grimaced and lifted a hand in apology to the driver she'd accidentally brake-checked.

The road she'd turned onto wasn't paved and had been

nearly hidden by low-hanging branches reaching out from either side of the drive, their long tendrils meeting and tangling with one another in a leafy embrace. She'd have admired their beauty if she wasn't so focused on avoiding potholes. The mix of hickory and oak trees filtered the harsh afternoon sun and gave off a secluded feel, even though they had just turned off the main road that led in and out of Rolling Brook.

"Where are we going, Rosie?" she asked as she crept along, keeping her eyes trained on the perilous road in front of her.

She'd already spotted several tree roots that protruded from the dirt, snaking up like eager fingers to ensnare unsuspecting passersby. Having experienced one flat tire, she wasn't eager for another.

Anna glanced in the rearview mirror and frowned at the cloud of dust obscuring everything in the direction they'd traveled from. If they did get a flat, it wasn't likely Officer Hottie would show up to rescue her. Not that she wanted him to. She didn't need another run-in with Mr. Perfect.

"It's the last stop on the tour!" Rosie's voice betrayed her excitement, and Anna chanced a glance at the older woman's face. Her green eyes shone, and her perfect dentures beamed in a wide smile.

Rosie's enthusiasm was contagious, and she smiled back, forcing thoughts of Luther out of her mind. "Great!"

She'd spent the last few hours driving around Rolling Brook with Rosie, visiting the properties the historical society owned or had a hand in saving. The list was extensive for such a young organization, and she was thoroughly impressed by her new colleagues. They'd done a lot with a little over the last ten years, and she looked forward to furthering their reach even more.

She was practically blinded by the sun's brightness when the trees parted. She blinked rapidly to clear her vision, then sucked in a breath and pulled to a stop. The sight of a crumbling farmhouse both entranced her and broke her heart.

Finding such a historical building intact was rare, even if this one was in rather bad shape. She had a soft spot for the rustic—buildings whose beauty was often overlooked because they weren't as showy or stately as the traditional antebellum homes people thought of when they heard the word 'preservation.' This farmhouse was made of logs and had to date back to the 1700s.

"Rosie! This is amazing!"

Rosie chuckled. "Yes, but there's more. Come on, keep going." She shooed her hand at Anna, who couldn't imagine anything topping that house.

She gave it one last look before continuing down the lane. The front porch may be hanging off, and part of the roof was collapsed, but the original timber and stone frame stood proudly. She envisioned the farmhouse wholly refurbished and turned into a venue for . . . something. She could see it as a place for events or weddings if there was more space. They'd need to clear out the brush and then build a large—

Anna gasped as the thing she had just been thinking of appeared before her.

A large red barn, its paint faded and worn away in spots,

stood in a field beyond the house. Surprised to find the grass mowed around it, she wondered if it was the society's doing when Rosie broke into her thoughts.

"Grand, isn't it?"

"Very." Before she could say more, Rosie gestured for her to park on a patch of gravel next to the barn.

As soon as the car had stopped moving, the sprightly older woman jumped out. Still a little dazed, Anna followed more slowly.

"How is this still here?" she asked in wonder, gazing around at the remnants of what had once been a thriving farm.

Rosie's white head swiveled toward her, and a grin split her face. She shrugged as she answered. "That's the beauty of this place, Anna. It's haunted, so everyone leaves it alone."

She couldn't help but laugh. She was no stranger to the idea of haunted houses in her line of work, but she didn't believe in them. "Well, that's good for us, I guess."

Rosie laughed, too. "Yes, it is."

"So what's the story with this place? I'm guessing the society owns it?" She twirled and shielded her eyes to look across the field at the house.

Behind it stood a couple of smaller outbuildings—sheds, which were likely kitchens or smokehouses at some point, judging by the chimneys. A pile of haphazard lumber that had once been a building and a rusted piece of farm equipment lay abandoned nearby. The whole place smacked of neglect.

"We do. The last surviving relative donated it to us about

a year ago. They didn't live on the property, of course. No one has since before I moved to Rolling Brook, which was in the 80s."

"It's got so much potential, Rosie. I can see it all fixed up. It'd be the exact thing Rolling Brook is missing—a large event venue."

"It certainly could be, dear, but we've had trouble getting an investor." She shook her head, and her coifed white waves bounced with the movement.

"Because it's haunted?" Anna grinned knowingly. "Why do people think that?"

"The rumor is this place was the site of the largest bootlegging operation in the county during Prohibition."

"Oh! I'd love to be able to corroborate that." She perked up at the idea of research.

"Well, and you might be able to. We've only begun to look at the property records. The massacre should be in the local papers," Rosie mused.

"Massacre?" Her jaw fell. She was having a hard time relating the idea of something so gruesome to the tranquil scene in front of her.

"Oh yes, nearly a dozen were killed. One of the gangs out of Chicago came after the bootleggers. Not sure why. They destroyed the whole operation and stole all the stills they found."

"So their ghosts wander here, waiting for revenge?" she smirked.

"If you believe in that sort of thing." Rosie smiled in response. "I'm not saying there's no such thing as ghosts, but I've never felt anything malicious here. This old place just needs some TLC."

"Yes, it does!" She rubbed her hands together. "Can we look inside?"

"The barn we can. The house isn't safe, though. Not in its condition. Going to need an engineer for that one."

Anna couldn't help a little squeal of excitement at the thought of exploring the barn. "Okay, let's open her up!"

Rosie pulled a massive set of keys out of her purse, which had to weigh as much as she did. Anna wasn't sure how she kept them all straight. She'd talk to Sandy about getting some realtor locks placed on the society's properties so the huge keyring wouldn't be necessary.

Rifling through them, Rosie landed on a large barrel key and used it to open the ancient-looking iron lock on the barn's side door.

Leaving the lock dangling, the older woman grasped the handle and struggled to pull the door open. Anna was about to help her when it gave way, sending Rosie flying backward into her arms.

"Rosie!" She stumbled back a step but was able to keep them both upright. Luckily, the older woman was petite like Anna and weighed next to nothing.

Rosie burst out laughing, and she joined in. When they'd settled down to the occasional giggle, the older woman said, "Thank you, Anna. I'd for sure have broken something if you hadn't caught me."

"You're welcome, but we better be careful. Do you want to come in or wait out here?" She glanced into the darkness of the barn's interior, eager to explore what lay within.

"You go on without me. I know what's in there. If you

open the main doors, you'll have some light. Otherwise, you need a flashlight." She smacked her hand to her forehead. "I completely forgot to bring them. My memory's not what it used to be."

Anna smiled. "That's all right. I can use the one on my phone."

Rosie nodded. "Oh, that's right. You do that."

"Be back in a few." She waved, then hit the flashlight button on her phone.

Holding it up in front of her, she stepped into the barn and was hit with the damp, musty smell of a place that hadn't been aired out in far too long. It filled her nose and slithered its way down her throat. As the cloying scent made her cough, she raised her arm to cover it, causing the light from her phone to bounce against the shadows with the movement.

When she'd got herself under control, she flashed the light around. She didn't scare easily, but the interior was pitch black. The beam from her phone didn't reach very far, and the thought of walking into spiderwebs she couldn't see was enough to have her heart racing. She hated spiders. Or anything that crawled, actually.

"Careful of the mice, hon," Rosie called from behind her, and Anna cringed.

Mice? Gross.

Praying none of the little vermin ran across her feet, she shuffled forward, flashing the light back and forth as she went. She knew she had to be getting close to the front double doors. If she got those open, there'd be plenty of light. And the creepy crawlies would scatter and hide.

When her beam caught on the metal of a crossbar lock, she smiled in relief. The double doors were locked from the inside with an old metal sliding latch. Shifting her phone to her left hand, she grasped the latch with her right and pulled. A screech filled the air as the lock slid, and she jumped back as the doors swung inward.

Sunlight filled the barn, and she spun around, curious to see what the interior looked like. To either side of her were two large stalls for horses or cows. She wasn't sure, but further, deeper, it was precisely what she'd been hoping for. Beyond the stalls, the barn opened into a large, vaulted room. A room where she could imagine parties being held or even wedding vows being read.

It was perfect. Well, almost. They'd have to install windows to let in some natural light that would brighten the space and help with the smell. She rubbed her nose and fought back a sneeze. Dust motes danced in the sun rays she'd let in, but she saw the potential. Cleaned up, it would be rustically charming.

Dreaming about how she would transform the barn, she walked outside and met up with Rosie. After they'd resecured the doors, they headed for her car. Before she climbed in, she took one last look at the farmhouse. It could be used for staging or even offices, while the barn would be the big draw.

She turned and snapped a few photos with her phone. It was the perfect large event venue Rolling Brook needed. She couldn't wait to start researching the property and drawing up a plan that would breathe new life into the place.

CHAPTER 4

Anna

Anna plopped down on her bed with a satisfied sigh. The white wedding ring quilt shifted with her movement, but the downy softness of the mattress cocooned her in comfort. Her room at the bed and breakfast was like stepping into another era, and she loved it. The antique furniture and reproduction wallpaper delighted her. It was decorated in pastels, blues, and yellows; today, her mood was as cheery as the room.

Touring the society's properties had been exhausting but also exhilarating. Excitement thrummed in her veins despite the ache in her feet. She should have changed into flats instead of walking around all those buildings in her heels.

Kicking off her favorite black Jimmy Choos, Anna flexed her toes and winced as the balls of her feet cramped. Reaching down to massage them, she froze at the knock on her door.

Who could that be?

She didn't know many people in town, and, so far, she'd only gone out for work, choosing to spend the evenings having dinner alone in her room, like the pathetic hermit she was.

Another knock sounded, and she rolled her eyes at herself. Walking to the door, she opened it, and her breath caught.

In a shaky voice, she asked, "What are you doing here?"

Luther grinned, and his dimples appeared. "Looking for you."

Her brain had shorted at the sight of those indentations, and it took her a moment to recover. "What? Why?"

"I needed to speak with you about the vandalism of your car."

"What vandalism? My car's fine. I was just using it." She frowned, her eyes narrowing on his silver ones. Why did it seem like he was laughing at her again?

"Your tire, Miss Hendricks."

"Oh." Her cheeks reddened, and she made her voice airy to cover the embarrassment of not understanding. "I wouldn't call that vandalism, but fine. What about the tire?" His eyes *had* been laughing at her.

"I've started interviewing people who attended the meeting, but I need to know if you'd like to press charges when we find the person responsible?"

"For a flat tire?" She shook her head. "That seems a little extreme."

Now, he was the one frowning. "It may seem like nothing, but if they know they can get away with a small act of vandalism, who's to say they won't escalate? Next, it might be keying the side of your car, or maybe they get bold enough and come after you."

As the possibility of what he'd said hit her, cold dread settled into the pit of her stomach, washing away the heat of embarrassment she'd felt earlier. "Oh."

"Look, Anna, I don't want to scare you—"

Too late for that.

"—but it's better to be cautious."

She nodded, not wanting to discuss it any further. "I'll press charges."

"Okay, well, good. I'll keep you updated with what I find out. In the meantime, . . . want to have dinner with me?"

She blinked, her tired brain confused at the change in subject. "Dinner?"

His grin flashed, and she wanted to sink into the well of his dimples.

What? She mentally scolded herself. *No, she did* not.

"Yeah. Have dinner with me."

She shook her head to clear it. Was this a joke? Was Officer Hottie asking her out?

Incredulous, she glared up at him. "Why?"

"Because my mom makes a mean meatloaf, and it'll be better than whatever you were going to have in your room."

She scowled, wondering how he knew that had been her plan. She needed to explore the town's food options, but eating out alone didn't appeal to her.

When the mention of his mom penetrated, her eyes widened. "Are you asking me to have dinner with your mother?"

"Is that weird?"

"As a first date, yes." She knew her face betrayed her, but, seriously, who did that? Or wasn't it weird because she'd already met his mother? The woman did own the bed and breakfast they were standing in.

Ugh, why can't I figure him out?

A smirk slowly spread across his face, and the silver of his eyes danced. "So, this is a date?"

She kicked herself for walking right into that one. If it wouldn't have embarrassed her further, she'd have groaned out loud. "No! I'm not going on a date with you."

"But meatloaf? Tonight?"

She wanted to refuse, but meatloaf sounded amazing since she'd been living off cold sandwiches from the corner grocery. Her treacherous stomach growled, and she had no choice but to agree.

"Fine. Because it's with Janet, it's not a date."

He coughed to hide a chuckle, and her eyes sparked. If he laughed at her, she would change her mind.

"Fine. Meet me downstairs in half an hour?"

"Fine."

She started to close the door, but he stopped her. "Oh, and Anna?"

Wary, she braced herself. "What?"

"You might want to"—he coughed into his hand again, then gestured at her face with a finger—"wash up."

She slammed the door and let out a squeal in frustration. It was impossible not to hear Luther's laughter as he walked away. Rushing to the oval mirror above the vanity, she looked at herself. There were smudges on her nose and chin.

Dirt or rust, possibly, from the locks?

She must have rubbed it on her face at the barn.

Fudge! Why am I always a mess when I run into him?

* * * *

Anna

After a quick bath, Anna changed into more casual clothes than her work suit. She'd already touched up her makeup from scrubbing the dirt off her face. Determined not to give Luther anything else to laugh at her about, she checked herself in the mirror one last time.

She'd pulled her hair into a half-pony and switched to understated jewelry. With her cap-sleeve blouse and jeans, she looked relaxed—normal. Not like she was trying to impress him. Because she wasn't, this *wasn't* a date.

Satisfied with her appearance, she took a steadying breath and headed down for dinner. When she reached the landing, she paused.

Luther waited for her at the bottom of the staircase. It was a strange meeting, like she was a debutante at her coming-out ball, as she descended the stairs toward him.

His eyes never left her, making a wave of self-consciousness almost cripple her and send her scurrying back to her room. But she straightened her spine when it threatened and persevered, refusing to let him get under her skin.

Once she'd descended, she held her head up and breezed past him without a word, only to stop after a few feet. She didn't know where they were having dinner with Janet.

Rolling her eyes at herself, she turned and put a cheery smile on her face to hide the inner turmoil. "Where are we eating?"

He hadn't moved from the bottom of the stairs. He stood hipshot with his hands in his pockets, watching her with a smile on his face. "You clean up nice."

The words felt more like an insult than a compliment. "Thanks?" she scoffed.

Luther chuckled. "I guess that didn't sound that flattering, did it? But I meant you look good, Anna, really good."

Before she knew what was happening, the smile left his voice, and he closed the distance between them. The silver of his eyes turned molten and seared her, melding her to the spot.

"Good enough to eat."

She stared, transfixed, as he lifted a hand to her face with practiced ease and brushed his thumb across her bottom lip.

The rough feel of it against her skin made her suck in a sharp breath. Heat flashed in his gaze at her reaction and arrowed straight to her core.

What is he doing to me?

"You know, your lips remind me of ripe strawberries."

She blinked in confusion. *Strawberries?*

She had to force herself not to lean into him when he bent down. His mouth hovered above hers, and she felt his next words as much as she heard them. "Can I taste them?"

"Wh-what?" she stuttered in surprise.

"I want to kiss you."

Her brain had turned to mush, but her body responded instinctively. The walls she'd built went up as fear overtook the desire, fogging her thoughts.

She stepped back, breaking the contact. "No."

He frowned at her. Was it any wonder? He probably wasn't used to hearing that word.

"Anna—"

"Ah! There you two are. Come and eat dinner. The meatloaf's getting cold." Janet came through from the direction of the kitchen and cut off whatever Luther had been going to say.

She was glad of the interruption, except she might have bolted and skipped the whole thing if his mother hadn't shown up. Now she'd be forced to sit through the meal with him after that . . . uncomfortable prelude.

Ignoring him, she smiled at his mother. "Thank you for having me."

Janet was short like Anna, and her round face glowed with warmth. She smiled and clasped her hands together. "Of course! I'm delighted you're joining us. It's quite a treat for me. I don't usually get to see this one"—she thumbed a hand at Luther, who was still frowning in her direction—"nearly enough."

He finally stopped staring at her and answered his mother with a grin. "What! I'm here every week."

She smiled at her son, and Anna couldn't help when the corners of her mouth lifted at the sight. Clearly, his mother was very fond of him, and they seemed close.

"Pfft." Janet waved her hands toward the kitchen. "Let's eat before it's only good for cold meatloaf sandwiches."

Anna hadn't entered the kitchen at the bed and breakfast before, and when she did, she was surprised at how normal it looked. She'd been expecting something in line with a commercial restaurant, but instead, the kitchen was homey. It was much more modern than the rest of the house, with dark granite countertops, a matching tile backsplash, and contrasting light cream color cabinets. But what struck her was the smell.

As soon as she'd entered, it hit her, making her stomach growl. The mouthwatering scents of cooked onion and tomato lingered in the air. "It smells amazing."

"Thank you." Janet gestured to a round dining table in the kitchen's eat-in area. "Have a seat."

She paused, surprised. Luther had pulled a chair out for her. She stubbornly didn't want to take the seat he offered but didn't want to cause a scene. After a prim "Thanks," she sat down.

He took the seat directly across from her, and she looked away, annoyed he'd put her in this position, literally and figuratively.

She was thankful when Janet appeared and placed a carving tray piled with meatloaf on the table. "Here we are. I've just got to get the sides."

Luther popped up at that. "Sorry, Mom. I should be helping."

She waved him back into his seat. "No, I've got it. Go ahead and dig in before it gets any colder."

"Are you sure?"

"Yes." His mom returned to the counter for the mashed potatoes and green beans while he served himself a slice of meatloaf.

He held his hand out for her plate, and she hesitated. She was capable of serving herself. She didn't need *his* help. "I can do it."

"I'm sure you can, but I'm trying to be polite here, Anna. Give me your plate."

"No." Maybe it was childish, but she was starting to like using that word on him.

He raised an eyebrow at her short answer. "Fine. Here." He offered her the serving fork, and their hands touched when she grabbed it.

A jolt of liquid heat raced up her arm at the contact, and she nearly jerked her hand away before she realized how strange that would make her look. Avoiding the stare she felt boring into her, she selected a piece of meatloaf and placed it on her plate.

"All right. Does anyone need anything? Ketchup? Extra butter?" Janet asked after she placed the last side dish on the table.

"I'm fine, thank you." She glanced up at Janet, who eyed the meal like a general surveying her troops.

"We're good, Mom. Sit down and eat."

Apparently satisfied, she gave a little nod and sat.

As they passed the food around, she asked, "So, how long have you been running the bed and breakfast, Mrs. Monroe?"

"Oh, please, call me Janet. And it's been, what?" She

looked to Luther. "Ten years now?"

He nodded, his mouth full of cheesy mashed potatoes. A little bit of which had ended up on his chin.

As his mother pointed it out, Anna had to hide her smile behind her napkin. It was nice to not be the one with stuff on their face. He swiped at it, and she turned her attention back to Janet.

"It's a wonderful spot. I'm enjoying staying here while I search for an apartment."

"Thank you." The innkeeper beamed. "How's that coming?"

"Not as easily as I'd thought." She frowned and fiddled with the tip of her fork. "There aren't many options, and what there are just aren't what I'm looking for."

"Ah. Well, what are you looking for?"

"I don't want to live in a box." She sighed, the low-ceilinged, cookie-cutter, box-like apartments being all she'd found so far. "It has to have character—*history*. And if I could find something in town or close to it, that would be perfect."

"Mmm," Janet hummed in agreement. "Those are hard to come by, but I'll watch for any vacancies."

"Thank you." She took a bite of her green beans and barely suppressed a moan. They were smothered in a decadent sauce that tasted heavenly. "Wow. These have to be the best green beans I've ever tasted. What's in the sauce?"

Janet blushed at the praise. "You're sweet, Anna. Thank you. It's a white wine butter sauce. Oh!" She popped out of her chair and rushed to the refrigerator. "I forgot the wine."

She was set to refuse it, knowing she had to get up early for work tomorrow, but when Janet brought the wine to the table, it was a rosé—her favorite.

One glass won't hurt.

An hour later, she'd gone through two glasses and was feeling pretty good. She'd started sipping her wine whenever she'd caught Luther staring at her. It helped ease the burn his eyes ignited in her. But that had led to too many sips.

At least her head felt clear, if a little lighter than usual. The meal had passed surprisingly quickly, with her conversing easily with Janet for most of it. His mom had tried pulling Luther into the conversation, but she was happy leaving him out.

Instead, she'd talked with Janet about the rehabilitation of the bed and breakfast and the historical society's current projects. She'd even found out Sandy's son had done most of the B&B's restoration work.

According to Janet, his carpentry skills were unsurpassed in the area. Now that she knew the beautiful woodwork surrounding them was his handiwork, she was inclined to agree. She was considering asking him for a quote on refurbishing the farm property she'd seen today when Luther's voice broke into her thoughts.

"You didn't have to make dessert too, Mom."

"I know I didn't have to. I wanted to. Besides, it's your favorite. Angel food cake with candied strawberries."

She blushed at the mention of strawberries and gulped wine to hide her embarrassment.

Of course, they're his favorite.

His foot tapped hers under the table, and her gaze shot to his. Looking at him was a mistake. His eyes were hungry, devouring her like she was the piece of cake. "Do you want dessert, Anna?"

The wine swam in her veins, and she used the liquid courage. Taking a steadying breath, she replied in an even voice, "No."

His eyes narrowed at her answer, the silver turning to smoke, and she could imagine the flames hidden beneath searing her. It felt as if they already were.

Under the table, her thighs clenched. She was hot, much too hot, as his eyes burned a path through her core.

"Oh, but you must! It's truly the best part of the meal." Janet broke their stare off and the tension by setting a plate of angel food with strawberries in front of her.

"All right, I will," she responded automatically, but her brain raced in fear at what Luther's gaze did to her.

She balled her fists in her lap, her nails biting into her palms. The pain helped clear her head, and she blinked, the dessert in front of her coming into focus.

It did look delicious, and she didn't want to hurt Janet's feelings. Taking another sip of wine, she ate the cake, avoiding Luther's eyes at all costs. He was trying to trick her with those bedroom looks, but she wasn't falling for that. Not again.

* * * *

Luther

Luther watched Anna as she hugged his mother. She'd

drunk three glasses of wine in less than two hours. While that might not be much for some, for a person her size, it was a lot of alcohol. She'd blow positive right now if he tested her, and he wouldn't be surprised if she were close to the legal limit.

She swayed a little when his mom released her, and he stepped closer, ready to catch her if she fell over. "Are you sure I can't help you with the dishes?"

His mom shook her head. "No, no, you're the guest. I won't have it." She smiled to soften the words, and Anna giggled.

"Well, thank you again. Dinner was fantastic."

"I'm glad you enjoyed it." She patted Anna's hand. "You're welcome anytime."

"Thank you."

"I'll escort you up." He wasn't sure Anna would make it up the stairs on her own.

At his offer, she spun around and glared at him. "That's not necessary."

Her words were starting to slur, making him think it *was* necessary. "I insist." He grabbed her arm and tucked it in his. "Let's go, half-pint."

As he dragged her away, his mom called "goodnight" after them. When they were out of the kitchen, Anna jerked her arm out of his with enough force to almost knock herself over.

She took a couple extra steps to keep from falling, then placed a hand on her head. "Uh-oh."

"Feeling dizzy there, Anna?" He grinned, and it was more than a little wicked. She'd given him the cold shoulder all night, so what if he was enjoying that she was tipsy? He hoped she'd drunk enough to have her regretting it in the morning.

She nodded, then hiccupped. Her beautiful gold eyes grew large, and she clamped a hand over her mouth. When another hiccup escaped, she burst into giggles.

"I think"—a hiccup—"I drank"—more giggles—"too much."

He wanted to stay annoyed with her, but she was just too cute in her inebriated state. Her laughter was infectious, and he chuckled along with her.

"All right. Come on, Giggles. Let's get you to bed."

"Okay, Officer Hottie." She giggled even harder at that.

"You think so, huh?"

She laughed more in response.

"Well, it's some consolation," he muttered under his breath. Retaking her arm, he steered her toward the stairs.

"Luther?" she said his name slowly as if she had to concentrate on pronouncing it.

"Yeah?" He was focusing on getting her feet to move. It felt like he was dragging her, and it would be easier to lift her into his arms. She couldn't weigh much, but she'd probably have a fit if he tried.

"Why'd you wanna kiss me?"

"Geez, Anna." He would have run his hand through his hair in frustration if he'd had a free one. "How 'bout we have this conversation when you'll remember what I tell you."

"I'll remember."

"No, you won't. You're drunk."

She stopped them halfway up the stairs and turned to him. Indignant, she punched a finger into his chest. "I'm not drunk."

"Sure you're not, Shortcake."

She was like a dog with a bone. "I'm not."

"Fine."

"Then tell me."

"No."

"Yes."

Damn, they were arguing with each other like children, but he couldn't help himself. "No."

"Yes!" she almost screamed.

"Shhh! Other people are staying here too, you know."

"Sorry. But I want to know."

She was so stubborn. He didn't understand why he liked that about her, but he did know he wanted to kiss her—badly. Her strawberry lips were puckered in a pout, practically begging him to taste them.

"You really want to know?"

She nodded.

He leaned in close to her mouth, and the scent of wine washed over him with her breaths. "Because I want to know what you taste like."

Her eyes glazed over, and she swayed toward him.

At her response, a zing of satisfaction spread through him.

Not so cold now.

Straightening, he captured those gold eyes and waited for them to clear. "But you're going to remember when I taste you, Anna."

She blinked, and a blush heated her cheeks. Turning away from his gaze, she continued their trip up the stairs.

When they reached her door, she rushed through it, muttering goodnight as she closed it in his face. It would be comical if he weren't so frustrated with her.

He couldn't remember the last time he'd had this much trouble with a woman. She'd refused his kiss, but he knew she was attracted to him. It didn't make any sense.

Maybe I moved too soon? he thought as he wandered back downstairs.

He hadn't meant to, but she'd looked so damn sweet in her cute top and jeans. Like the girl next door, the girl you wanted to bring home to Mom. Not that the snooty Anna in her business suits didn't heat his blood, but this Anna . . . this Anna made him want more than a quick roll in the sheets.

That wasn't something he'd looked for in a long time, which meant it was something he'd have to think about *before* he made another move.

CHAPTER 5

Anna

Anna jerked upright at the sound of her alarm, then moaned and grabbed her head. An army of drummers beat a steady rhythm behind her eyelids. Blindly, she reached for her phone on the bedside table. She had to stop that terrible noise before her head exploded.

When she'd succeeded in cutting off the blaring, she cautiously opened her eyes only to squint them against the sunlight streaming in her window. It was the soft light of early morning, but it was still too bright in her current state. She swallowed and coughed. Her mouth was as dry as the Sahara.

I haven't been this hungover in years.

Knowing she had to get ready for work, Anna slung her legs over the side of the bed and braced herself to get up. Water and ibuprofen would make this all better, and they were waiting for her in the bathroom. She stood up slowly, careful not to jar her head, then staggered to salvation.

When she'd made it to the ensuite, she was perspiring from that little amount of exertion. She gripped the edge of the porcelain sink to steady herself. Raising her head, she winced at her reflection in the brass-framed mirror above the vanity. Sweat dewed her upper lip, her complexion was a little green, and she had dark circles under her eyes. Her hair was even worse. It looked like small creatures had made a nest in it overnight.

Why did I drink all that wine?

She started to berate herself but then remembered Luther was the reason she'd drunk so much. It was much more satisfying to place the blame on him. If he hadn't been all, all . . . she frowned at her lips in the mirror as the memory of him hovering so close to them came back to her. She started to lift her fingers to the spot his thumb had brushed. Then she came to her senses.

Ugh! The man was driving her crazy. He'd been pushy, and she hated being pushed. But she'd put him in his place, hadn't she? Things were a little fuzzy, but she remembered him asking to kiss her and her telling him no. Watching his face fall at that simple word had been so satisfying.

Men like Luther whose egos were as big as their . . . she blushed at the direction of her thoughts.

Muscles. She was going to say *muscles.*

Those men needed to know not every woman would fall at their feet.

Realizing she was wasting time stewing over him, she pushed off the sink and started the shower. She needed to get moving, or she would be late for work. Digging through her medicine bag, she found the pain reliever pills and swallowed two with a cup of water from the sink. She gulped down a second cup and noted her complexion had improved . . . some.

Last night, she'd been foolish to drink so much, but she vowed not to make that mistake again. She had to be on her guard around Luther, which meant having complete control of her faculties. Because she'd learned a long time ago that looks could be deceiving and behind his eye-candy exterior was likely just another conceited jock who enjoyed playing games with women. Games she refused to play.

* * * *

Luther

When his alarm rang out, Luther sighed, rolled over, and hit the off button. It had been a restless night, and he'd been awake for the last half hour, staring at the plaster medallions on the ceiling of his home. He lived in a Victorian-era house that had been converted into three apartments. His comprised the third floor of the building.

A sleepy smile spread across his face. It was the sort of place Anna was looking for, and he knew she would love the decorated ceiling. He'd paid little attention before now, having chosen the place because it was close to the station and within walking distance of the local hangout, Nick's Tavern.

But this morning, he saw the marble fireplace, the transom lights above the doors, and the brass wall sconces above his bed with new eyes. There was charm here—

history. Just like Anna wanted. Images of her swirled amidst the turbulent sea of his thoughts.

Prim and proper in her tailored business suits, frowning at him as he teased her, then cute and uninhibited as she'd relaxed at dinner with his mom.

Which Anna would he get when he took her to bed?

His blood stirred, and he groaned, throwing an arm over his eyes as if that would block out the picture of her swaying toward him, those bright strawberry lips begging to be kissed. The woman was driving him crazy.

He was good with women, except for this one. He couldn't figure her out, and he wanted to. For the first time in a long time, he wanted to know every inch of her—inside and out.

Honesty was important to him, so he wouldn't lie, even to himself. But owning up to the need to get to know her, to caring enough about her to want to get close, pierced him with a stab of anxiety. He rubbed at the spot above his heart as an ache started there.

That particular organ hadn't been involved in a relationship in a long time, and the thought of risking it again made his whole chest tight with fear. The last time he'd given his heart, the recipient had tossed it from a five-story window and then run over it for good measure. That was almost ten years ago, but thinking about the possibility of it happening again had him ready to break out in cold sweats.

He supposed it was laughable that the tiny brunette scared him. But she did. The question he had to answer was, could he face his fear?

Anna's big gold eyes and the secrets she hid there made him want to. That much he was sure of. But he had other secrets to uncover first, including who slashed her tire, and he wasn't going to find out lying in bed.

Already exhausted, he grunted and felt like an old man as he forced himself to get up and get ready for a long day of legwork.

* * * *

Anna

Despite the rough start to her morning, Anna had a very productive day. She was beaming at the file on her computer screen, which she'd spent all day perfecting. Excitement over the plans she'd drawn up for the abandoned farm property thrummed in her veins.

Yeoman's Hall, she was calling it. She hoped the townspeople would like the name and were willing to drum up half as much enthusiasm as she felt for it. Then, they'd be getting somewhere. For that to happen, though, she needed Richard's help.

A movement caught her eye, and she glanced up.

Speak of the devil.

"You wanted to see me?" Richard leaned against her door frame.

"Yes. I need a strategy for engagement." She smiled. "That's where you come in." She gestured for him to take the seat in front of her desk.

Community outreach was his forte, and she needed someone who'd lived in town longer than five minutes to help her figure out the best way to present her plans.

While he moved to sit down, she exited out of the document and ejected the thumb drive it was saved on.

Handing it to him, she asked, "Can you look over my proposal for the Cooper farm property and give me your ideas on how to get the community involved?"

He accepted the drive with a raised eyebrow. "I didn't realize we had plans for the Cooper property."

She grinned, and her golden-brown eyes twinkled as bright as stars. "We didn't, but when Rosie showed it to me, I knew it needed to be our focus. If we can get the community involved with something like this, they'll be more open to the other changes Rolling Brook needs. Maybe then we can turn some of those neglected buildings on the edge of town into offices and rentals."

"If the mayor doesn't have them torn down first," Richard muttered.

Her stomach dropped. Despite the muttering, she'd heard him loud and clear, and his statement killed her buzz. "Is there something you're not telling me?"

He sighed and pinched the bridge of his nose before meeting her gaze. "Only that Mayor Landstrom is set on revamping that whole area into some modern-looking mixed-use development with retail, offices, and apartments all in one spot."

She wanted to groan in frustration, but she kept her composure. She'd known the mayor was pro-modernization. "Is there already a development plan for the area, or is it just conjecture?" They had time to change the mayor's mind if nothing had been approved.

"I don't believe so." He shook his head, and his dark waves ruffled with the movement. "*But,* it is part of the campaign she ran on. As far as I know, nothing has been submitted to the committee for approval just yet."

Anna sighed in relief. "Good. We still have a chance to win that battle, then. It'll help if we can get the town behind us, and I think the Cooper property could be a good start with that."

"All right," he said with a nod.

"Thanks, Richard." She smiled in dismissal and turned her attention back to her computer screen. She had an email to send before she called it a day.

As she pulled up her inbox, she noticed he hadn't left. She looked over at him. His stare bore into her, and she couldn't read his expression.

Confused that he was still waiting, she asked, "Was there something else?"

He blinked, then smiled, clearing his gaze. "No. You surprise me, that's all."

"Oh? What do you mean?" She clenched her hands and gave him her full attention, bracing herself for what he might say. He'd been dancing around her since they'd met, and something about him tended to get her hackles up.

He chuckled, and it set her teeth on edge. "I know this is your first real job, and . . . you're not floundering."

She kept her smile pleasant even though her claws threatened to come out. "You thought I'd flounder?"

"The county wanted to hire someone with the right degree. They didn't care about how much experience that person had." Giving a slight shrug, he smiled to soften the remark, but her face had already reddened in embarrassment.

She was struggling with how to reply when he stood and waved the thumb drive. "I'll take a look at this tomorrow. I'm sure with my experience, we'll find a way to sell your project to the town."

She forced a smile through the tightness that had taken over her body. She tensed for a fight, but Richard left before she could respond. When he was out of view, she exhaled and felt some of the tension leave her muscles.

Shi—take mushrooms!

She was no stranger to veiled insults, but those had hit home. Did he have a problem with her background or the lack thereof?

Agitated from the exchange, she pushed to her feet and moved to open the window. She was desperate for some fresh air, but of course, it was painted shut.

Fudgesicles!

Spinning around, she grabbed the closest thing that would serve as a fan—a folder on her desk. The stale air moving across her face did little to cool it. She'd spent years training herself not to cower when faced with confrontation, but that didn't make her any more comfortable with it.

People were not her strong suit. She understood books and records but had no idea why Richard felt the need to rub her lack of experience in her face.

Huffing out a breath, she dropped the useless folder and sat down. She had to work with him no matter how much he irritated her.

Resigned to the fact, she slumped further into her Louis XVI desk chair. The upholstered arms embraced her in soft burgundy comfort, and she ran a finger along the laurel leaves carved into their ends. This job was too important to let him ruin it for her. She'd have to find a way to win him over, one way or another.

* * * *

Luther

Luther cracked his neck from side to side as he unlocked the door to his apartment building. He'd just finished his nightly three-mile run, but his body had almost let him down with the lack of sleep. He'd been about to give in and walk the last mile, but he'd forced himself to push through the weariness that was as much from his revolving thoughts as from his long day.

Stepping inside, he stared at the curved staircase with its wreath handrail and turned balusters. Right now, it looked as tall as Mt. Everest. His legs were tired, and he needed a second to slow his breathing before climbing three flights of stairs.

He'd been so busy starting the investigation that his conversation with the pizzeria worker had prompted he hadn't drunk enough water, and he felt the lactic acid building up in his muscles.

His legs had gotten a workout before starting the run since he'd spent most of his afternoon running around town. He'd gone to the Shoppes again, then to the bank and Town Hall to look at property records. A cramp seized his left leg, and he winced.

He leaned a hand on the banister for balance to stretch it out. After all that digging, he'd learned less than expected. The suspicious activity investigation was going about as well as tracking down who slashed Anna's tire.

He switched to his right leg as his thoughts went back to Anna. It seemed he'd spent half the day trying to focus more on work and less on her. He'd talked to a few more people who'd attended the town hall, but it hadn't produced any leads. None of them had noted anything suspicious. The lack of information was beginning to make him wonder if he'd been wrong and maybe she *had* just run over something sharp.

He shook his head to clear it and started up the stairs to his apartment. He must be exhausted if he was questioning his instincts. The tire had been deliberate; he was positive. All he needed was the camera footage to prove it, but he still had to wait on that.

Unless there's a way, he could get it sooner . . .

He was distracted enough by his thoughts that he nearly tripped over the boxes in his path when he reached the second-floor landing.

As he stumbled, Cassie came out of her apartment carrying another box. Her blue eyes grew wide when he grabbed the railing to steady himself. "Oh! Sorry, Luther!"

"Hey, Cass. What's with the boxes?"

Her long blonde hair fell over her shoulder as she set down the one she was carrying. "I'm leaving." She straightened and gave him a shy smile. "Shane asked me to move in with him."

He smiled at the young woman he'd known since kindergarten. "That's great, Cass. Congratulations." Cassie and Shane had been dating for about a year, so this news wasn't surprising.

He gestured to her boxes. "Do you want any help with these?"

Please say no. He wasn't sure his legs would make it if he had to climb all those stairs again.

She chuckled. "It looks like you already got your workout. Thanks anyway, but they're not heavy."

"What about with the rest of your stuff?" He braced himself. If she were moving everything out now, he'd find the strength, somewhere, to help her.

"Thanks for the offer, but not yet." She tucked a flaxen strand behind her ear as her cheeks pinked with excitement. "I'm just taking a few things over for now. My lease isn't up until the end of the month."

Relief flooded him, and he nodded in response. He was set to leave when a thought occurred to him. "Hey, Cass? Do you know if there's already someone lined up to take the apartment after you? Because I know someone who'd be interested."

"Oh, that would be wonderful! It'll help Lennie get over the sting of me leaving when I already told him I wanted it for another year."

"Great." He grinned at the prospect of having Anna in the same building. It wouldn't be so easy to avoid him then, would it? "I'll let her know, and you can schedule a time to show her the place."

"All right." Cassie nodded and bent to pick up her boxes.

"I'll see you later then."

"'Night." He jogged up the last flight of stairs. The anticipation of delivering to Anna exactly what she'd been searching for was a shot of adrenaline that burned all signs of fatigue out of his body. He now had the perfect excuse to see her again.

CHAPTER 6

Luther

Luther leaned against the mahogany reception stand while waiting for Anna to arrive. He'd already been up to her room and found she wasn't back from work yet. Although . . . glancing at his watch, he noted it was half-past six. Maybe he'd missed her, and she'd gone out to dinner. Frowning over that possibility, he crossed his arms and decided to wait ten more minutes before calling it a loss.

The weekend had dragged on as he waited to tell her about the apartment. He'd thought he would have the chance on Sunday, but when he'd come for dinner with his mom, Anna hadn't been in her room.

He was happy to have some good news for her since he'd gotten no more information on the vandal who slashed her tire. After talking to everyone who attended the meeting, he was no closer to a suspect. It's possible the person who damaged the wheel hadn't gone to Town Hall for the meeting.

They might have been there just for Anna.

His frown deepened, and a knot formed in the pit of his stomach. He didn't like entertaining that idea, but it *was* a possibility—one he couldn't ignore.

"What are you doing here?" Anna's voice startled him out of his thoughts.

He straightened, then turned around to see she had entered from the back door of the bed and breakfast. His mood lifted at the sight of her in her black business suit. She wore a skirt today instead of trousers, and he enjoyed the glimpse of legs. They were creamy and surprisingly long for someone so short.

Grinning now, he asked her, "Working late today?"

"Unfortunately," she muttered, and he thought he saw a scowl cross her face before she turned away.

"Hey? Everything okay?" He stepped toward her, and she lifted her gaze, pinning him to the spot with glaring eyes. She was angry all right, and now it was directed at him.

"Fine," she snapped.

Luther hesitated. He wanted to tell her about the apartment, but she was clearly upset about something. Would pushing her on it make things better or worse? Searching her face didn't provide him an answer.

He blocked her path as he debated with himself, and she raised an eyebrow at him. "You're in my way."

At that, he grinned. If haughty Anna was back, maybe he could tease her out of her bad mood. "Well, I did have the inside track on the exact type of apartment you were looking for, but if you want me to go . . ."

Her eyes softened, but her posture was still defensive as she shifted her weight and crossed her arms over her chest. "Oh? Where is this apartment?"

"Ah-ah-ah. The information's going to cost you." He grinned and mirrored her posture.

Her eyes flamed, and her hands flew to her hips. "Really, officer? Because that sounds like extortion to me."

His brow wrinkled in worry at the anger radiating off her in response to his teasing. "Anna, what's wrong?" he asked, dropping the act.

Her shoulders slumped, and she looked away. "Nothing."

Seeing her so distressed made lead settle on his chest. Whatever it was, he wanted to help her. Stepping closer, he reached for her chin. She tensed when he touched her, but he didn't let go.

Turning her to face him, he soothed, "It's 'nothing.' Tell me what's got you so upset."

"It was a misunderstanding. That's all." It sounded like she was trying to convince herself as much as him.

"What was a misunderstanding?" He brushed a strand of hair off her face, and her eyes widened. Before she could put distance between them, he reached for her shoulders and rubbed. "It might help to talk about it." His eyes caught hers and held, his voice coming out gravelly as he pleaded, "Tell me."

Her muscles were tight under his hands, so he worked on relaxing them. As he kneaded, he watched her inner struggle. "Come on, tell me," he coaxed.

When she let out a low sigh, a small smile curved his

lips, happy she'd given in.

"Richard."

His body went on alert at the name, and his hands stilled. "Richard Cartwright?"

He'd had a bad feeling about the man, but his search into her co-worker's background had come back clean.

"Yes, he's helping me with a project and . . ." Her gaze turned glassy, and she bit her lip.

The movement drew his eye, and he wanted, badly, to soothe the spot with his tongue, to taste her and drink all her worries away, but that wasn't what she needed right now. "What did he do, Anna?"

Her cheeks flushed, and she avoided his gaze. "We were having drinks to discuss the project, or so I thought."

She was killing him, dragging this out. His mind raced with scenarios, all of which caused his blood to heat. He was ready to track down Cartwright and beat the shit out of him, and he didn't even know what the man had done yet.

Working to keep his voice and his hands gentle, Luther lifted her face to his. "What happened, Anna?"

"He hit on me, that's all." She gave a slight shrug, but she wouldn't look him in the eye.

Is she embarrassed, or is it something else?

He could hardly blame Cartwright for trying when he'd wanted Anna in his bed since he'd met her, but something felt off about her explanation. "Are you sure that's all? I need to know if he did or said anything that crossed the line."

"He didn't." She shook his hands off, and he sighed,

realizing she wasn't going to tell him anything more.

"Okay, but if Cartwright ever tries . . ." Red coated his vision, and his hands clenched into fists at the thought he couldn't finish. "Then tell me," he managed in a gruff voice.

"Fine, I will." Regaining her composure, she stood up taller, quirking an eyebrow at him. "Now, what about this apartment?"

Luther blinked. He'd almost forgotten about it in his worry over Cartwright. Shaking those thoughts from his head, he forced a smile. "Well, it just so happens I found exactly what you're looking for."

"Oh really?" she scoffed. "I think I'll be the judge of that."

Damned if that didn't make him chuckle. He liked it when she was feisty. "I'm sure you will." He winked, then held his hand out. "Give me your phone."

"What? I'm not giving you my phone." She took a step back, ignoring his outstretched hand.

"How am I supposed to give you the contact number and address then?" he teased.

She rolled her eyes. "For starters, you could write it down, or, here"—she pulled her phone out of her work bag—"just tell me, and I'll add it to my contacts."

"Do you have an answer for everything?" he smirked at her stubbornness.

Her eyes narrowed at him, and he admired the way the gold glowed when her irritation with him rose. "Do you have to mock me?"

He frowned. Is that what she thought he was doing? Tease her, yes, but he would never mock her. "I'm not mocking you."

"Well, it feels like it to me."

"Trust me, Anna. Mocking is the last thing on my mind when it comes to you."

When he took a step toward her, she swallowed and stepped back. His need for her was a hunger gradually eating away at him. It left him starving and half-crazed from deprivation if he dwelled on it. He dropped his gaze to her lips.

What he wouldn't give for one kiss, one little taste.

She cleared her throat, and he blinked, bringing his eyes back to hers. "The apartment?"

A slow smile started as he contemplated her moving into the apartment under him. He wanted her under him in other places too . . . like his bed.

Luther swallowed, throat dry from that tantalizing image. He was so thirsty for a taste of her, but he was going to quench his thirst sooner or later.

Swallowing down his need, he gave her Cassie's number and told her the street address.

"Thank you." She looked ready to bolt, but he was still blocking her path. "Goodnight, Luther."

Moving aside with a grin, he told her, "See you later, Anna Hendricks."

As she rushed by, he caught a whiff of her scent.

Skittles. It made his mouth water.

Yeah, he was going to get that taste.

Making a move or not was no longer the question. What he had to figure out was how to make her crave him, too.

* * * *

Anna

Anna shut the door to her room and collapsed against it. She was so tired. The events of the evening had left her emotionally drained.

Men! If it wasn't Richard, it was Luther. Why couldn't they leave her alone?

The last thing she'd wanted after drinks with Richard was to run into Luther. She shuddered as she thought about what had happened with her co-worker.

He'd hit on her, but it had felt like more than that. Or perhaps it had just been the way he'd done it. Men had shown interest in her before, but Richard's had seemed . . . menacing almost.

She was probably overanalyzing things, but she'd caught him ogling her more than once with a feral look in his eyes. Then he'd "accidentally" touched her and made her skin crawl. Anna shook her head. However he'd meant it to come off, she dreaded seeing him at work the next day.

She pushed herself off the door and locked it, ensuring she would be left alone for the night.

Usually, the sight of the beautifully restored antiques decorating her room served to brighten her mood, but tonight she barely noticed them. Silent tears leaked as the unfortunate meeting with Richard replayed in her head.

He'd made it clear he didn't see her as an equal by hitting on her during their "work" drinks. She'd been excited to discuss his community engagement plans, but Richard had only given vague responses to her questions, choosing instead to focus on her.

She rolled her eyes. She didn't need or want Richard's attention on anything to do with her *except* the farm project. She wobbled to the bed with legs that felt like jelly and sunk into it. Her whole body felt weighed down by her current situation and the memories clinging to it.

She curled into a ball without any thought of wrinkling her designer suit. Staring up at the plaster molding on her ceiling, it wasn't the decorative laurel leaves she saw. Her vision turned inward as the events of the evening blurred into flashes from her past, creating a turbulent image she wished, desperately, to escape.

She'd been a freshman in college, sheltered, naïve when Dan had taken an interest in her. An upperclassman, a leader of his fraternity, and an all-star on the baseball team, he was the jock Anna could never forget. She'd been beyond flattered by Dan's attention, immediately falling under the spell cast by his baby blues. Two short weeks later, she'd been in love, ready to give him any and every part of herself.

Snorting in derision at her stupidity, she rolled over and squeezed her eyes shut. It didn't stop the memories, though. They continued to play out behind her eyelids, and she couldn't look away like a rubbernecker at the scene of an accident.

She saw the party where she'd bolstered herself with a glass of punch spiked with who knew what to calm the nerves that threatened to overwhelm her, knowing it would be the night she lost her virginity. She'd known Dan was experienced and didn't want to disappoint him. He'd been so patient and gentle with her up to that point.

A sob escaped her throat, and she placed her hands on her stomach against a spear of pain that sliced through her. How abruptly he'd changed. The sting of his betrayal tore through her as flashes of that ill-fated night bombarded her. She hugged herself tighter as she fought against the memories—against a past she couldn't alter.

That night, the world she'd lived in came crashing down on her. Dan had taken her virginity and broken her heart into so many pieces she was sure it was impossible it would ever be whole again. He hadn't loved her as he'd said. It had all been lies—an act to get her into bed so he'd win the bet he'd made with his frat brothers.

Now, she cried loud, noisy tears for the girl she'd been. Dan had taken much more than her virginity, but she'd vowed never to be so naïve again.

When the memories released her, she dried her tears and dragged herself to the bath. She needed a hot soak in the claw-foot tub to cleanse herself of the stench of the past—of the smell of despair hanging about her in a cloud as heavy as the plague.

She may not be able to go back and save that naïve college girl, but she wasn't about to make the same mistake twice. Scowling, she turned the water on as hot as it would go, then started shedding her clothes. She tossed the Valentino suit aside with hands that jerked in anger.

Luther may not be after her because of a bet, but she had no delusions about what he wanted from her. He'd gotten jealous when she'd mentioned her drinks with Richard. It was apparent Luther thought someone else was sniffing around his territory.

As if he has any claim on me!

She didn't need any man, and she especially didn't need one like Luther. Distracted by thoughts of him, she stepped a foot into the bath and yelped before jerking it back out of the scalding water. Rolling her eyes at herself, she turned on the cold and waited for the tub to reach a reasonable temperature before sinking into it.

At least Luther had given her some useful information—unlike Richard. She wasn't looking forward to seeing him at work tomorrow, but if she set up an appointment to view the apartment Luther told her about, perhaps the anticipation would get her through whatever uneasiness was bound to exist between them.

Sighing, part in frustration and part in contentment, Anna leaned back and closed her eyes, letting the comfort of the bath envelop her.

She'd deal with tomorrow . . . tomorrow.

CHAPTER 7

Anna

Anna pulled up in front of the address Luther had given her and smiled. A Victorian-era building that would have been considered a mansion in its time stood before her. It was painted a bright yellow accented with white trim. The cheery color stirred the excitement simmering in her veins.

She already had a good feeling about the apartment. The location was excellent, only a few blocks off Main Street. She'd be able to walk to places, and though there wasn't as much to do here as in D.C., where she'd grown up, it was a start. Stepping out of her car, she crossed her fingers and sent up a quick plea that the inside would be just as charming.

If this panned out, and she wanted it to, she'd have to thank Luther properly. She'd been rather snippy with him last night, but her mood had been far from even after the fiasco with Richard. Thinking of Richard again brought a frown to her lips.

She climbed the steps to the front porch, trying to focus on its architectural details as she ran her hands up the carved wooden railing. Still, the distraction didn't soothe the nerves on edge from her coworker. Thankfully, he'd been assisting with a program in a neighboring town today, and their paths hadn't crossed. She wasn't looking forward to it when they did.

A shudder racked her body, and Anna took a deep breath, shaking off the memory from the previous evening, before lifting a hand to the brass-coated doorbell on the front of the house. Even this tiny thing was decorative—a swirling fleur-de-lis wrapped around the straightforward button.

Smiling at the delicate detailing, she pushed the buzzer. When she didn't hear the typical chime of the bell, she frowned and tried again.

Still nothing.

Undeterred, she knocked on the heavy wooden door and waited.

No response.

After several moments, she knocked louder, sticking her ear to the door this time to see if she heard anyone moving within, but she was met with silence.

Stepping back, she pulled her phone out to check the time. It was now four o'clock—the time she'd set up to see the apartment.

Annoyance was starting to override the feeling of excitement she'd had since arriving. She huffed out a breath and dropped her phone back into her bag. Should she wait outside? Or . . .

She stared at the antique brass knob. It was located in the center of the door, flanked on either side by recessed panels.

Should she try it? Would it be unlocked?

Her eyebrows furrowed, and she chewed her lip as she debated. Curiosity won out, and she tried the doorknob. It turned easily in her hand, and the door slowly creaked open. Nervous now, her pulse jumped as she stepped inside.

"Hello!" she called, hoping someone would answer so she felt less like an intruder. "Cassandra?"

The woman had told her the apartment was on the second floor, so Anna started up the steps, thinking perhaps she'd meant to meet her at the apartment at four, not simply at the building. The staircase curved with the structure, and her fingers danced along the handrail as she ascended, lovingly tracing the craftsmanship that was so hard to find in contemporary construction.

When she reached the second-floor landing, she paused. She was here to look at Apartment Two, and the brass number "2" was on the door in front of her. Crossing her fingers again, she knocked on the door and prayed Cassandra would answer.

After less than a moment, the door opened to reveal a beautiful blonde with eyes the color of cornflowers. "Hi! You must be Anna?"

She smiled in response but fought the urge to fidget with her hair. She probably looked a mess compared to the effortlessly put-together woman in front of her. "I am. And you're Cassandra?"

"Oh, just Cassie, please. Here"—she stepped back and opened the door wide—"Come on in."

A wide grin spread across Anna's face as she entered the apartment. The charm was there in the polished hardwood floors, the picture railing, and the detailed molding around the doorways and windows, and that was just what she saw from the main room.

"It's lovely." Her heart raced, and she was eager to see the other rooms.

Cassie chuckled. "I'm glad you think so, but let me show you the rest."

She followed Cassie as the young woman led her through a dining room complete with a chair rail and wainscoting to a kitchen, which, despite being small, had been updated and housed a dishwasher—a rare find in a historic home.

At the sight of it, she was ready to sign the lease. She mentioned this to Cassie, who laughed and told her she knew the feeling. Washing dishes by hand was the absolute worst.

Anna relaxed in Cassie's company and thought, despite their differences, they could be friends. It would be nice to know at least one other person in town who was close to her own age.

They toured the bath, which was also updated and had a stackable washer/dryer combination. It would be wonderful not to have a shared laundry. That had gotten old fast during college.

The last room was the bedroom. There was only one in the apartment, but it was spacious and even had a fireplace. She drifted toward it in a daze, drawn to the beautiful tile surrounding it. The design was a mix of pinks and burgundies swirling together in a pattern akin to marble. Someone had built a carved wooden mantle with a mirror around the hearth and columns with decorated ends graced either side.

She ran her hand along it as Cassie commented, "The fireplace has been converted to gas, so it's serviceable."

At that, Anna smiled. She couldn't wait for the weather to turn so she could curl up by the fire with a book and a cup of hot chocolate.

Guess I'm taking the apartment, then.

Not that she hadn't planned to as soon as she'd stepped through the door.

Giving the fireplace one last caress, she turned to Cassie. "Dishwasher, laundry, and a fireplace? I'm sold."

Cassie surprised her with a squeal as she clasped her hands together. "That's wonderful! You don't even know." She shook her head. "This helps me out so much. Lennie, he's the landlord," she explained, "he was going to be so upset. But if you take it, it won't be vacant." She shrugged and grinned. "And no harm, no foul."

Anna smiled back. "Well, it's perfect. I'm glad it works out for both of us."

"Absolutely!"

When Cassie headed back into the living room, she followed.

The blonde talked over her shoulder as she went. "I'll be out in a week, and it'll be all yours. I'll give you Lennie's contact information and let him know the turnover is going down. He's a little ornery, so don't be surprised if he's rather gruff with you at first. It takes him a while to warm up to people."

"I know what that's like," she muttered.

Cassie stopped and turned. "What was that?"

"Nothing. That doesn't bother me." She avoided eye contact as she took the last few steps to the door and picked up her work bag from where she'd left it. "Do you want to just text me his information?"

"Works for me." Cassie opened the door and smiled. "It was nice to meet you, Anna. I'm glad you're taking the apartment."

"Thanks. Me too."

She stepped through the door, but Cassie stopped her. "I think you'll like the neighbors too." She winked. "Luther, you know, is upstairs, and the other, George, is an artist. He's a quiet one. Keeps to himself."

She'd frozen at the mention of Luther. Her brain stuttered over the realization that this was his building. "Luther lives here?" she squeaked out through a throat gone painfully dry.

Now Cassie frowned. "Yes. Don't you know him? I assumed when he mentioned . . ." She trailed off at the shock Anna knew had to be on her face.

Of course, he hadn't told her he lived here. *He's a liar, just like Dan.*

"I know him, but he omitted that detail when he told me about the apartment."

"Are you all right?" Cassie placed a hand on her arm.

She blinked and felt her skin heat. A burning was

starting in her gut and fanning its way up her chest into her face. She smiled around gritted teeth. "Fine. Thanks again for the tour."

"Of course. I'll send you Lennie's info."

"Great." She nodded and turned away.

Walking blind, she started up the stairs to the third floor. Her vision had gone red, and she needed to find Luther.

At the knowledge he had tricked her, the anger she'd been walling up too long overpowered shame and embarrassment. It burst through the dam she'd built to contain it, and she was helpless to stop the flow. If he thought he could manipulate her, he had another think coming.

* * * *

Luther

Luther was in the process of shedding his uniform when there was a knock at the door. Today had been a rough one. He'd delved deeper into the investigation of the suspicious activity and what he'd found . . .

He rubbed a hand over his mouth, but the sour taste lingered. Right now, he wanted nothing more than to slip into the shower and shut his brain off. Sighing, he buckled his belt and walked to the front door, not bothering to put his shirt back on.

Opening it, he found Anna on the other side. With one look at her, the fatigue that had plagued him for the last hour evaporated like steam over a hot stove.

"Well, hello there, Anna." He looked her up and down, distracted enough by her tailored blouse and snug-fitting skirt not to notice the expression on her flushed face.

"You lied to me!" She poked him in the chest, and he was surprised enough by her outburst to let it push him back a step.

Confused, his eyebrows rose, and he rubbed at the spot where she'd stabbed him. Her little fingernails were sharp. "What are you talking about?"

"You didn't tell me this was your apartment building!"

She was yelling at him from the hall, and he winced, hoping his neighbors didn't overhear and come to investigate. He grabbed her arm and tugged her inside to avoid making more of a scene.

Before he had a chance to respond, she jerked out of his grip and stabbed at him with a finger again. "You're a liar, and I—"

He clamped a hand over her mouth. "Anna, will you calm down? What does it matter if I live here? It's not my apartment that's available. I knew Cass's would be perfect for you. That's why I told you about it."

His rushed explanation didn't have much effect. She was glaring daggers at him, and her chest heaved hot breaths against his hand.

"Ow!" he yelped, pulling his hand away.

She'd bit him. *Hard.*

"You are so, so *infuriating!*" she yelled.

He stared down at the bite mark on the inside of his palm. At least she hadn't broken the skin, but was she crazy?

Who bites people except for toddlers and Mike Tyson?

"You bit me."

"You deserved it."

He felt his own anger start to stir. He'd done her a favor, and this was how she was going to repay him. "I didn't lie to you."

"Oh really? A lie by omission is still a lie." She hurled the statement at him with enough disdain to boil his anger over.

"You want complete honesty, Anna? Is that it?" He bit out through clenched teeth.

"Yes!"

"Fine!" Her eyes widened as he advanced, backing her up against the door. "Then I'll tell you I want you so bad, I can hardly breathe past the hunger clawing at my throat." He rested his hands on either side of her body, caging her in.

Her breath hitched, and a thrill rushed through him.

"Your lips." He stared at them, his own lips aching to touch the ruby-red temptresses. "I dream about them, about what they'll taste like."

Leaning down, he gripped a handful of the hair by her neck and lifted it to his nose. "And your perfume." He breathed in deeply, and her eyes had glossed over when he looked at her. "It drives me crazy."

He bent his head again and angled his lips toward her ear. "I want to lick every inch of you, everywhere that scent has touched. It lingers, and I can smell it even when you're not around."

Having said his piece, he released her hair and leaned

back, keeping her caged in with a hand on either side of the door above her shoulders.

He'd succeeded in silencing her. When she swallowed, he traced the line of her neck with his thumb. "Nothing to say to that, Anna?"

Her pulse fluttered under his hand, and he leaned down, his cheek nearly touching hers as he breathed her in. "Honesty goes both ways." He grazed his lips across her cheek to her ear lobe.

At her soft sigh, he whispered against her ear. "Tell me you don't want this too. Tell me, and I'll stop."

She didn't say anything, so he placed an open-mouthed kiss on the spot just below her ear. When she shivered, he smiled against her reaction like the Cheshire cat and ran his hands up her lithe little body. She melted into him and made his pulse jump with need.

Groaning, he skimmed the outside of her breasts with his fingers and watched her eyes close. When her lips parted, Luther leaned in, gliding his mouth across her jaw before pulling back just enough to look into her face.

"Anna." At his voice, she opened her eyes. They were dark and heavy-lidded. "Do you want me to kiss you?"

Her gaze fell to his mouth.

Yeah, she wants it.

On a grin, which had his dimples popping out, Luther goaded, "Be honest."

CHAPTER 8

Anna

Anna had lost the ability to think. All she could do was feel while her heart pounded in her ears. The fire from her anger had cooled into a liquid warmth that sat low in her belly. She stared at Luther's mouth. It was moving, but she didn't catch the words.

Lost in a sea of so many new sensations, she lifted her hands to trace the dimples in his cheeks. The scruff there tickled her palms and made her catch her breath.

At her sharp intake, he stilled her hands. When she met his eyes, they were as dark as a storm cloud.

"Anna," his voice begged while his eyes raged at her, "kiss me."

Kiss him? Where?

Her eyes fell to his shoulders and the muscles of his chest. Why wasn't he wearing a shirt?

Wanting to touch him there, she placed her palms on his chest, admiring how hard it was. She ran her hands over him, feeling her way down his bare torso.

He shuddered under her touch, shocking her. She stopped and pulled her gaze to his. Had she hurt him?

Lightning from the storm in his eyes flashed at her, and his voice strangled as he begged, "Kiss me, Anna."

His hands caressed her back and sent shivers down her body. Standing on her toes, she leaned into him. As her chest pressed against his firmness, a bolt of heat arrowed to her core, making her whimper. She closed her eyes against the feeling and searched for his lips with her own.

When they connected, the thunderstorm she'd seen in his eyes erupted. He growled and grabbed her, lifting her until he had her legs wrapped around his waist. With her back pressed into the door, he devoured her with the force of a hurricane, and she was helpless to do anything but let the wind and rain barrage her.

His tongue swept inside her mouth, and he tasted familiar, almost . . . like candy. He caught her lip between his teeth and sucked. She moaned, and he answered by moving his hands to her breasts. Her head fell back with a long sigh when he caressed her nipples. What was he doing to her?

It feels too good.

Her skirt bunched around her hips, and when she arched her back, pressing her center to his, a bolt of heat pierced her. She gasped, and he swallowed it with his lips and tasted her some more.

A kiss? She'd never been kissed like this.

A pressure built within her, and she thought it might burst if he didn't stop.

"Luther!" She tore her mouth free. Her breath rushed over her swollen lips as she searched for the eye of the storm in his dark gaze.

She needed a measure of calm, a quiet port, to understand what was happening.

He blinked and dropped his forehead to hers. His breathing was labored, but his voice was gentle when he spoke. "Sweet. You taste so sweet, Anna."

I do?

"You taste like, like, Skittles," she said as she recognized the familiar candy flavor.

He chuckled and leaned back to look into her face. "You smell like them."

"What?"

"Skittles. They're my favorite candy, and you"—he leaned in and sniffed at the base of her neck, licking his way up her throat—"smell like them."

His mouth on her wasn't helping clear the fog from her brain.

"I want to taste more of you." He nipped at her jaw. "Come to bed with me, Anna."

The word 'bed' was like getting hit in the face with sleet. The cold, wet precipitation woke her up, and she stiffened in his embrace. "Put me down. Now."

His head flinched back at the force of her words, but he complied. With her feet on the ground, she adjusted her skirt and avoided eye contact with him.

How had she let this happen? She'd let him trick her *again.* Shame heated her face, and she wanted nothing more than to escape. Where had she left her bag?

As she glanced around for it, Luther spoke, "Anna—"

"Don't!" She didn't want to hear whatever he had to say. *No more lies!*

"Look, I'm sorry if that was too fas—"

"Stop!" She wheeled on him with the force of a tornado. She'd never been more charged up and confused. There was an electricity sparking through her, threatening to lash out at any moment.

His face fell at her shout, and when he opened his mouth to speak again, she ran, afraid of what she might do if she didn't get away from him. On her way out the door, she about tripped over her work bag.

As she scooped to grab it, she thought she heard him mutter, "What the hell just happened?" She wondered the same.

Chest heaving, she raced down the stairs on shaky limbs, desperate to flee the scene of the crime.

* * * *

Luther

Luther stared after Anna in a daze. For such a little thing, she packed quite the punch.

In more ways than one.

He'd thought tasting her would satiate the hunger, but it intensified it. Now, he wanted her more than ever.

Damn, she was sweet.

And spicy.

He rubbed his jaw, wondering what had made her flip out on him like that. She'd been so pliant, so willing in his arms. It had been clear she wanted him too, but then she'd cooled like someone had flipped a switch, and suddenly he was dealing with her evil twin.

He wasn't sure what had caused it, but either way, she sure as hell owed him an explanation.

Shutting the front door, he walked back to his bedroom to change. He'd give her time to cool off, but this wasn't over, far from it.

He switched into running shorts and grabbed a water bottle on his way out the door. His system was all kinds of confused. A run would at least work off the excess adrenaline pumping through his veins since he wasn't getting the other form of release he craved.

CHAPTER 9

Anna

Anna had never been much into zombies but felt she'd pass as one right now. Taking a sip of her coffee, she sighed. After what had happened with Luther, she couldn't sleep. Her thoughts had kept her tossing and turning. One minute, she'd hated him; the next, she'd hated herself. Maybe he'd tricked her, but she'd let him do it. She'd let him seduce her, just like she'd let Dan. The difference was, with Luther, a part of her ached for him to do it again.

Fudge on toast!

She was a mess. Groaning, she lowered her head to the steering wheel. She was dragging her feet. It was time to go to work, but she was sitting in her car, berating herself as if it would change anything.

Gawd, I'm tired.

When she'd been fortunate enough to drift off last night, she'd dreamt of Luther, and the dreams had been all too real. The kiss they'd shared played on repeat every time she'd closed her eyes, and she'd wake from dreams wanting him to do it again, only to hate herself for it.

Sighing, she lifted her head and made one last check of her reflection in the visor mirror. There was little she could do to hide how drained she looked. Her usually pale complexion was wan, and she had dark circles under her eyes that were bloodshot from crying. She'd tried to cover it up with concealer but only partially succeeded.

I should've taken a sick day.

Even thinking that made her feel weak, she refused to let Luther, or any man, make her feel that way. Determined to push him out of her mind, she slammed her car door and headed to work. With any luck, she'd be in before the rest of the team, avoiding the concerned looks and questions bound to come her way.

Too bad fate had other ideas.

"Ah, there you are, Anna." Richard's voice grated on her overly wound nerves, and she had to take a deep breath before turning to face him.

He must have been in his office because he stood behind her in the hall. She'd been mere steps away from her sanctuary and cursed the universe for being so cruel.

"Good morning, Richard." She didn't bother to try to smile. At this point, it would likely turn into a grimace.

He took a step toward her, and she stood her ground even though the sight of him made her skin crawl. "Are you feeling all right? You look rather . . . pale."

"I'm a little under the weather . . . probably best not to come too close," she added with a smirk of satisfaction. *That's right. Stay away from me.*

Of course, the arrogant jerk didn't heed her warning. He took a step closer, his expression feigning concern, but it contrasted with the sharp look in his eyes. "I'm sorry to hear that. If you'd like, I could handle things for today while you get some rest."

He'd like that, wouldn't he? For her to turn over power to him.

Well, not going to happen, slimeball.

"Thank you for the offer, but I'll be fine." She nodded and turned away, ready to get started on the list of things she needed to get done today.

Turning her back on Richard was a mistake. He stopped her progress with a hand on her shoulder, and she flinched, unable to hide her revulsion.

"Don't touch me." She swung around to face him, the force of her anger bringing color to her cheeks.

He held both of his hands up in a show of surrender. "Whoa," he said with a smile, "someone's a little prickly. I just wanted to talk to you about the farm project before you dive into other things."

"Oh." She relaxed—a little. "All right, then. Come in."

She entered her office and was relieved when he sat in the chair across from her desk—away from her. She could handle this if he wanted to discuss the project, and he wouldn't bring up what happened the other night.

She sat at her desk and turned on her computer. "Okay, Richard. What do you propose for Yeoman's Hall."

He leaned back in the armchair, steepling his fingers as he grinned at her. "You know, Anna, I don't work for free."

"Excuse me?"

"I'm a consultant. I offer my services for a fee. Now, with you"—his gaze lingered on her chest before coming back to her face—"the fee could be paid in many ways."

Her face blanched. "I'm sorry, but are you implying . . ." She couldn't say the words.

He leaned forward, and she instinctively shied away from him. "Pretty little, Anna. You know exactly what I mean."

"Get out!" She'd meant to shout it, but it came out more like a squeak.

"Still prickly, I see." He rose and hovered over her.

She melted into her chair. *Please, go away.*

He didn't. "If you want this project to succeed, you'll reconsider. The fee stands, but . . . I wouldn't wait too long." He winked at her, and she couldn't help but shudder in response.

When he left, she tried to move, but she was frozen. Her mind rebelled against the conversation she'd just had. A part of her wondered, or rather, hoped, she was still dreaming.

She felt dizzy as her thoughts scrambled around in her brain. Richard had hit on her over drinks two nights ago, and though it had been more provocative than a simple pick-up line, she hadn't expected this.

Was he doing this as payback? Because she'd rebuffed him? Did he think he could coerce her into doing something she'd refused to do willingly?

With each question, her stomach clenched, and she felt nausea working its way up her throat. She gasped for breath and pushed to her feet on a hard swallow. In two quick strides, she had her door shut and locked. Leaning against it, she hugged herself as the other night with Richard replayed in her head.

The accidental brush against her breast as he'd reached for the drinks menu, the hand on her thigh when he'd wanted her attention, the leering looks. She'd written them off at first, thinking she was being overly sensitive—overreacting even. But blatantly asking her for sexual favors . . .

She gagged and lunged for the wastebasket. Mercifully, her stomach was empty. She spat into the bin, but the sour taste in her mouth remained. He wasn't going to leave her alone, so what was she going to do about him?

* * * *

Luther

Luther jumped at the knock on his window. He'd been staring at nothing, lost in thoughts of Anna again. Ever since their kiss, he couldn't seem to stop, not even when his head needed to be on the job.

Looking up to see who'd rapped on his window, he nodded at Sergeant Jameson, who motioned for him to unlock the door. He did, and Sarge climbed into the passenger seat.

When he sat, his red curls brushed the canopy. "Damn, tin can. You know you can take one of the SUVs."

Luther laughed. The Dodge Charger suited him just fine. "Yeah, but Suzie's more my kind of gal." He lovingly rubbed a hand along the dash.

Sergeant Jameson rolled his eyes at Luther's nickname for the cruiser. "Fine. Make this quick, then, Monroe. What have you found?"

He sobered, a frown marring his expression. He'd asked the sergeant to meet him in a field on the outskirts of town because he wasn't sure who they could trust at the station. "It's bad, Sarge. The SAR? It's legit." He tapped on the steering wheel with nervous fingers as he thought about his investigation into the Suspicious Activity Report. "The pizzeria barely scratches the surface. It looks like that whole development of shops—maybe others too—are all part of the scheme."

"Fuck!" Sergeant Jameson scrubbed at his face. "This is going to blow back on the whole town."

He swallowed. "Yeah, and . . . someone's providing top cover."

"How do you know?"

"I found other SARs, but someone had buried them."

"Dammit! That's why we're meeting in the middle of nowhere?"

Nodding, he added, "Do you think, I mean it could be the reason Haines brushed it off . . . what if he's involved?"

I don't know who to trust.

Sergeant Jameson's jaw clenched, and Luther searched his face.

Apart from you.

"Fuck, maybe. Don't breathe a word of this to anyone, but keep doing what you're doing. If we're going to bust this thing up, we need proof."

"10-4, Sarge."

He expected the sergeant to leave, but he started muttering to himself, "Fucking, Dillon. I'm blaming this on him. As soon as he leaves, the shit hits the fan."

He grinned despite the gravity of the situation. Lieutenant Redland had recently accepted a captain position in a neighboring district. He would have been another man Luther would've had no hesitation in trusting. At present, the vacated billet sat empty, and their captain was far from ready to fill it from the ranks. He would be okay if he found out their captain was dirty. There was no love lost there.

"Yeah, let's hope it's a small pile of shit."

Sarge sighed. "In my experience, Monroe, it rarely ever is."

CHAPTER 10

Luther

"Is this your plan? Keep showing up here until I agree to go to bed with you?"

Luther tensed. He'd been leaning against the reception stand again, waiting for Anna to return from work, but the tone of her greeting didn't bode well for him.

Turning, he pushed off the stand and took a couple of steps toward her. "Come on, that's unfair."

"Is it?" She crossed her arms and stared him down. "Why are you here, Luther?"

He ran a hand through his hair, mussing the blonde spikes. Maybe he should've given her more time to cool off. "Can we talk?"

"I was under the impression we *were* talking."

So, it's going to be like that.

Sighing, he told her, "Look. I'm not going to say sorry for that kiss. Not when it was"—he caught her eyes and made sure she saw what it did to him—"mind-blowing."

She gulped.

"But I'm sorry I rushed you." Unable to stop himself, he took another step closer and reached for her. Brushing the back of his hand across her cheek, he added in a murmur, "We can go as slow as you want, baby."

She flinched, and he dropped his hand. Her eyes spat fire at him as she said, "I am *not* your 'baby'."

He frowned. The evil twin was back. "Fine. Sorry."

"Do you mind?" She bit out through a forced smile.

"Mind what?" He was trying to keep up with her moods.

"You're in my way," she hissed at him. "Men are always in my way," she mumbled.

"I'm not moving until you tell me what happened yesterday. Why are you pushing me away when you clearly want—"

The slap of her hand against his dimpled cheek cut off the rest of what he'd planned to say. The strike was hard enough to make his face sting and his jaw tighten in anger. "Dammit, Anna!"

"Oh my god!" She clamped her hands over her mouth. Her eyes were as wide as saucers, and she appeared as surprised as he was that she'd slapped him.

She dropped her hands and started shaking her head. "I'm sorry. I'm so sorry. I can't do this. I—" Her face crumpled, and she burst into tears.

He cursed under his breath. This wouldn't look good if his mother or another guest walked in. He gently touched her arm, and when she didn't try to slap him again, he used it to steer her up the stairs to her room.

When they reached her door, he tried the knob, but, of

course, she'd locked it. Glancing at her, he slid the work bag off her shoulder. She was a sobbing mess. "Anna, where's your key?

"What?" It was a watery question as she sniffled and turned to look at him.

"The key to your room?" He opened the bag and pointed it toward her.

"Oh, it's—" She pointed to a small, zippered pocket before looking at him. "Your face is red," she whined in between sobs.

"Yeah, it stings a little."

That made her cry even harder. *Good job, Luther.*

Wanting to get her out of the hall, he unzipped the pocket and retrieved her room key. She rushed inside when he opened the door—straight to the adjoining bathroom, which she promptly closed in his face.

Frowning after her, he shut the door to her room, then set her bag down by the vanity she'd turned into a desk. He wasn't leaving until they talked this out. No matter what she wanted.

Knocking softly on the bathroom door, he said, "Anna, please let me in." He needed her to . . . in more ways than one.

"No. Go away!" Her voice muffled through the door, but he heard the tears she couldn't seem to stop.

"I'm not leaving until you talk to me."

When she didn't respond, he sat down and leaned his back against the door. "Please, Anna."

She didn't answer, and he questioned his sanity. Why was he pursuing a woman who'd not only been pushing him away but had slapped him? He wanted her, yes. But was it worth it?

If she hadn't sent him mixed signals, maybe he'd believe she wanted nothing to do with him. As it was, he was confused and wanted answers. But more than that, he was worried about her. He wanted to know what was bothering her, to help her through whatever it was. If that meant sitting here for the rest of the night, so be it.

* * * *

Anna

Anna leaned against the bathroom door and slid to the floor. Sobs racked her body, and she was helpless to cut them off. She hugged her knees to her chest while her thoughts swirled in a turbulent whirlpool that threatened to drown her.

How could she have done that? She'd never struck anyone in her life.

And she wasn't even mad at Luther, not really. She was mad at Richard. Thoughts of him made her cry even harder until she was choking from the lack of air.

Luther must have heard her struggling because he pounded on the door. "Anna! Are you okay? Please talk to me!"

But she couldn't, not after what she'd done.

Unable to face him, she slumped over until her overheated cheek pressed against the cool tile of the floor. She curled into a ball, and eventually, the tears slowed.

Maybe coming here was a mistake. Maybe she should

look for a new job in the morning. She wasn't sure she could handle working with Richard.

And Luther—a sob bubbled up again as she thought of him. He wasn't likely to kiss her again after she'd slapped him.

Crap on a cracker!

She bolted upright at the realization she'd assaulted a police officer. Didn't people get arrested for that? She feared hyperventilating as visions of jail time began to swim before her eyes.

She clutched at her chest when breathing became difficult. She'd have to apologize again. She couldn't go to jail. Her parents had already dismissed her for her life choices. She was supposed to marry well and continue the Hendricks political legacy, but instead, she'd chosen a career that had nothing to do with politics. At least not at the level they were used to. It was a sore spot between her family.

If she got arrested, they'd disown her for good and cut her off. She'd have to pay back her student loans. Her heart rate accelerated. She'd never be able to afford it!

In a panic, she pushed herself to all fours. A politician's daughter couldn't get arrested. It would be a black mark, one she wouldn't be able to come back from. She had to make things right with Luther before that happened.

She tried to steady her breathing, but it refused to cooperate. Forcing herself to stand, she had an errant thought she was having a breakdown, but she shooed it away and reached for the doorknob. "Luther!"

He nearly toppled into her as the door swung back. In

panic mode, she dropped to her knees beside him. "Are you all right?" Her voice rose with the question.

"What?" he asked as he stood, pulling her to her feet. "I'm fine. I was propped against the door. Are *you* okay?"

He searched her face, and it had to look like a mess. She hadn't even thought to fix her makeup.

She managed to nod at him, but her breathing was still unsteady. Working to get it under control, she blurted, "Don't arrest me! I'm so sorry I hit you. I didn't mean it. Please forgive me."

"Arrest you? Why would I arrest you?" His brow furrowed in confusion.

"Because I assaulted a police officer."

At that, he blinked, then he burst into a laugh.

She wasn't sure what was so funny, but she hoped that meant he wasn't planning to take her to jail.

When he kept laughing, she started to wonder if he was the one having a breakdown. "Luther?"

He looked at her and tried to stop. "I'm sorry,"—he managed around chuckles—"I just"—he laughed again—"what am I going to do with you?"

Her face blanched.

"No, I didn't mean—" He wisely cleared his throat around another chuckle. "Relax, if I arrested every woman who slapped me, I'd—"

She raised an eyebrow at him, and he stopped, coughing into his hand.

"—never mind."

Watching his face, she started to relax. He wasn't angry with her. Instead, he looked . . . relieved.

"What's going on with you, though?" He stepped toward her and swiped a thumb under her eye to catch a tear she hadn't felt fall. "You can talk to me, Anna."

Can I? She searched his eyes. They were open, unguarded. In the waning light filtering into her room, the light blue hue had turned to a soft gray, offering her the comfort of a cozy blanket. He'd told her to tell him if Richard crossed the line. What if he could help her?

She took a deep breath. She wouldn't find out unless she asked.

* * * *

Luther

"It's Richard."

Luther's whole body tensed at Anna's statement, and his hands clenched into fists. "What did he do?"

"At work this morning . . ." When she trailed off, he held his breath. The suspense allowed his thoughts to run wild. If Cartwright hurt her . . .

He ground his teeth and cautioned himself to stop jumping to conclusions.

She sighed, her shoulders drooped, and he hated that she looked so strung out. He vowed whatever it was, he'd help her with it.

"Richard implied if I wanted his help with the project, there were certain"—her voice tightened, and she looked away—"concessions I had to make."

Again, his mind raced to assumptions he didn't like. He worked to keep his voice calm despite the frustration building from her drawing the explanation out. "What kind of concessions?"

She brought her gaze back to his, and he saw the answer he'd been dreading. "You know what kind."

His lip curled in disgust as his blood pressure spiked. "Cartwright tried to bribe you for, for . . ."

Damn! He couldn't say it. The thought of Cartwright bribing her for sexual favors had nausea rolling through his stomach, and he swallowed against the sour tang of it rising to burn his throat.

"Yes. But . . . I'll handle it."

Her voice was anything but confident, and he lost control of his words. "Handle it!" he yelled. "I hope you fired his ass!"

She winced. "Technically, he doesn't work for me. He's a consultant for the county. I can file a complaint, but who knows how long that will take to do anything."

He took a deep breath and forced himself to calm down. "I'm sorry. Anna, come here."

He grabbed her and pulled her close. As her small body melded into his, some of the tension gripping him slipped away. She fit perfectly in the crook of his arm, and he wanted to shield her from the Cartwrights of the world. It was pitiful, wrong—so wrong—she'd had to deal with that kind of behavior in the first place.

As much as he wanted to go after Cartwright, he was a cop. He couldn't go around threatening men because they hit on his girlfriend.

His thoughts stuttered. *Girlfriend?*

He swallowed and tried it out again. *Girlfriend.*

He liked the way it sounded as he rolled the title around in his head. Anna, however, probably wouldn't be thrilled he was thinking about her that way.

Now, he understood the anger behind her slap, but he was still unsure why she was so determined to push him away.

As she pressed her cheek against his chest, he stroked her hair. The movement of the soft strands sent her smell wafting into his nostrils, and he closed his eyes, breathing in deeply. Damn, he wanted this woman. Her scent was intoxicating, and he wanted to drink it in, drink her.

"Thank you." Her murmured words broke into his thoughts, and he reminded himself that wasn't going to happen—yet.

"I'll talk to him, but you need to file the complaint." An idea started to form, and he grinned. Yeah, he'd talk to Cartwright. They'd have a *conversation* about how he was still a suspect in Anna's vandalism case.

"I know." She sighed and pressed against his chest, but he wasn't ready to release her. "I'll do it tomorrow."

"Good." And he'd visit Cartwright tonight.

"Luther?"

He was still stroking her hair. "Yeah?"

"You can let me go now."

She tilted her head up at him, looking into those golden-brown eyes, his hand stilled. He didn't want to let her go. He wanted . . . his gaze fell to her lips, those beautiful strawberry lips that tasted so sweet.

When her breath hitched, his stare flew back to hers. He saw the same need that hounded him shining in her golden eyes. Leaning down, he whispered against her lips, "Can I kiss you, Anna?"

Those plump red lips parted ever so slightly, and she nodded before closing her eyes. Not wanting to scare her off again, he kept his hunger in check, kissing her as gently as his need would allow.

She let out a soft moan when his lips brushed hers and opened for him. He accepted the invitation and swept his tongue in her mouth. Her sweetness flooded his senses as their tongues danced, and the beast in him, starving for more of her, taunted him to take it.

With one hand, he molded her against him. At the same time, the other cradled her head, his fingers tangling themselves in her soft brown locks as he continued to drink in her candied confection flavor.

When he felt his control slipping, he freed her lips and buried his head in the curve of her neck. He wanted this woman something fierce, and her bed was right there.

He groaned as he fought against the desire to take her— now. She wasn't ready, and if it had been merely sex, he wanted, maybe he wouldn't have cared, but it wasn't.

With Anna, he wanted more than one night, so he had to wait. But waiting wasn't easy.

With one last deep breath, he took in her scent, the perfume that haunted his dreams, and stepped back, releasing her before he made the wrong move. "I should go."

At his words, her gaze clouded and she bit her lip. He couldn't tell what she was thinking. His own thoughts warred within him as his focus again fell to her mouth.

When she turned away, he blinked and shook the lust from his head. She opened the door to her room, and he followed her.

With one last soul-searing look, he drank her in. "Goodnight, Anna."

As he walked away, he couldn't help but wonder if he'd made the right choice.

CHAPTER 11

Anna

Anna closed her eyes and leaned her forehead against the door to her room. She still felt Luther's lips on hers. Remembering how gentle he'd been, she touched a finger to them in a daze. How different this kiss had been from their first. Before, she'd been swept away in the storm of his passion, while this time . . .

This time, she'd been floating on a soft, fluffy cloud, the sun's rays warming her slowly from the inside out.

Sighing, she pushed herself off the door. Her lids felt heavy, and her body was spent from all the crying. Too tired to think of dinner, she flopped on the bed. As she sank into the downy mattress, her mind returned to Luther.

She wondered why he hadn't tried to take more from her than just a kiss. When he'd pulled away and told her he should go, she'd panicked, afraid she'd done something wrong. For that fleeting moment, she'd wanted him to stay. The desire surprised her. She hadn't wanted anyone since

Dan, and with Luther . . . the pull was so much stronger. The way he'd looked at her as he left . . .

Her blood heated as she replayed that look. Anna groaned and rolled over. The more he kissed her, the more she craved his mouth on hers.

Her stomach cramped against the opposing signals her brain broadcasted. Did she like Luther or not?

She didn't want to, but . . .

Did I misjudge him?

He'd stayed for her, even after she'd been so horrible to him, and then he'd offered her comfort. Not only that, but he'd offered his help. If he warned Richard off and she filed the complaint, perhaps the slimeball would leave her alone.

She clung to that hope, knowing it would get her through the next few days. On a yawn, she closed her eyes. Exhausted from the emotional rollercoaster she'd been riding and the lack of sleep from the night before, she drifted off amidst her revolving thoughts of Luther.

** * * **

Luther

Luther pulled up in front of Cartwright's house and glared at the quaint Craftsman bungalow. The man lived in a historic neighborhood where many of the houses dated to the 1920s. For some reason, the beauty of the home made him even angrier. A man like Cartwright didn't deserve a place like this.

The light brown color of the brick contrasted prettily with the bright red shingles hanging under the pitch of the gabled roof. A large picture window trimmed in white with exposed brackets held up a matching red flower box stretching the length of it. The box showcased a riot of colors: yellow, purple, white, and pink blooms that shone with a soft light in the glow of the setting sun.

Scowling, he rechecked the address, but it confirmed he was in the right place. Taking a calming breath, he reminded himself what the goal was here. He needed to get Cartwright to back off by scaring him, not pissing him off enough that he retaliated against Anna. Which meant he had to handle this as a cop and keep his cool.

He climbed out of the police cruiser and shook his shoulders. It didn't ease the tension in his muscles, and he gritted his teeth. The image of Cartwright asking Anna for sexual favors was eating away at his resolve.

As he climbed the steps to the red front door, he counted the space between his breaths until he slowed them down. It was a trick he'd learned at the academy that helped him return to a calmer state.

After a few slow, deep breaths, he pounded on the door. It didn't take long before Cartwright answered it.

His hands clenched into fists at the sight of the man. He'd rolled up the sleeves of his white button-up shirt but still wore his tie and dress pants. How relaxed Cartwright looked contrasted starkly with the adrenaline rushing through Luther's body.

The asshole tipped his head to the side, his dark eyes carefully blank. "Evening, officer. Is there a problem?"

He bared his teeth in a smile that couldn't hide his disgust. "Why do you assume there's a problem?"

Keep your head, Luther.

Cartwright returned the smile, and his eyes mocked him. "A social call, then?"

"No," he paused, his nostrils flaring. He was losing grip on the anger he was trying to contain. "I understand Miss Hendricks has had some trouble with you."

The bastard's expression didn't falter. "I'm afraid I don't know what you're referring to."

"You know exactly what I'm referring to." The threads of control Luther had hold of whipped out. "And I'm here to remind you we still haven't found the vandal who damaged her car, which occurred at the meeting *you* attended."

Cartwright's eyes bugged out. "Are you threatening me, officer? Isn't that—"

His pulse pounded in his ears as the fury he wanted to unleash whirled in his veins. "No." He stepped closer and lowered his voice, the brusque growl a promise of violence to come. "I'm *warning* you. Leave her alone, or you'll find yourself facing more than the prospect of being fired."

Cartwright's face flushed red, and he cursed himself for angering the man. "I'm a suspect, then?"

"Yes. I'm watching you." His hand went to the gun at his hip. "Tread carefully."

Cartwright's eyes flared, then fell to the gun. He started to close the door, but Luther slammed his hand against it.

"Was there something else, *officer?*" The man emphasized the title, his mouth twisting in derision as if it were an insult.

"Stay away from Miss Hendricks," he whisper-growled.

"You've made that clear."

"Good." He let go, and the door shut in his face.

Dammit! He wasn't happy with the way that exchange went down.

He'd succeeded in doing the opposite of what he'd wanted—pissing off Cartwright instead of scaring him. How the man would respond worried Luther. His stomach clenched at the thought of Anna having to deal with the consequences of his actions.

He'd lost his cool.

The rage at seeing Cartwright and the inability to touch him was still simmering in his veins.

He was usually laid-back and remained unruffled in charged situations, but now he couldn't find his calm.

Climbing into the cruiser, he sat staring at the cheerful bungalow as his hands clenched on the wheel. If Cartwright so much as breathed in Anna's direction, he would haul his ass in. If he couldn't find something to charge him with, he'd at least hold the bastard until he was afraid enough of going to jail that he'd leave her alone.

Luther forced himself to take several deep breaths and relaxed his hands. His knuckles were white in their death grip on the wheel. Slowly, his breathing returned to a normal rhythm, and he grasped the threads of control that had gone flapping in the wind of his anger.

Starting the car, he drove away, all too aware he couldn't undo what had just happened. He'd have to check on Anna tomorrow to make sure Cartwright heeded the warning because, after this screw-up, he wasn't sure the bastard would.

CHAPTER 12

Anna

Anna sat at her desk, massaging her temples. She'd woken up with a headache from her sob session the evening before, and it had gotten progressively worse over the course of the day. Not surprisingly, it had escalated with her stress level. She'd spent most of the morning getting the complaint filed against Richard, and that whole process had caused the headache to flare up.

Sighing, she dropped her hands. The rubbing had little effect, but she worried that if the pain continued, she'd be in full-blown migraine territory.

At the knock on her door, she jumped. Sheesh, she was tense. After everything with Richard, she'd taken to keeping the door closed, hoping to avoid him as much as possible. She hadn't seen him today and prayed it wasn't him at her door now.

"Come in," she called, sitting up straighter and pasting

a smile on her face.

When Sandy walked in, her smile grew, and her muscles relaxed. "Hi, Sandy."

"Anna. Hon." Sandy stalked to the front of her desk. "I'm worried about you. You've been holed up in this office for days. Is everything all right?"

She tensed up again, her expression falling as she said, "Richard and I aren't seeing eye to eye on something, and I thought it best to keep my distance."

The older woman's bright blue eyes bore into Anna as she studied her. It had her fighting the urge to squirm. What is it they say about a mother's intuition? She felt like Sandy saw right through her thinly veiled answer.

On a blink, the woman's eyes softened, and she smiled. "Well, lucky for you, he's not in the office today. But I was thinking, if you need some fresh air, I could get ahold of Jake, and we could go out to the Cooper farm. I know you need more measurements for your project. And it'd be good to get his contractor's eye on what you were thinking for the place."

At the thought of escaping and avoiding Richard, Anna beamed. The dark cloud that had been hanging over her all day evaporated. "That sounds like an excellent idea! Why don't you give Jake a call and let me—"

She stopped talking as the ringing of her phone intruded. Sandy nodded at her to take it and moved to leave, but she waved the woman into the chair in front of her desk as she answered the call, "Hello."

"Anna Hendricks?" an unfamiliar woman's voice asked.

"Yes."

"I'm calling from Mayor Landstrom's office. The mayor requests a meeting with you this afternoon."

She wanted to roll her eyes. *Politicians.*

They believed everyone should be at their beck and call. "Oh, well . . . I have plans. Can we schedule this for tomorrow?"

"I'm afraid not, Miss Hendricks. The mayor would like to see you right away."

She sighed. "All right. Fine."

This is my luck lately.

"Can you come to Town Hall in half an hour?"

"Sure." Resigned, she absently rubbed at the headache that had reawakened.

"Thank you. She'll see you then."

"Great."

"Goodbye."

"Wait! What is this about?" *Ugh!*

She should've asked that sooner. The woman had already hung up.

After she disconnected, she stared at Sandy. The older woman's blue eyes were concerned, her expression pinched. "The mayor wants to see you?"

"You heard?"

Sandy nodded.

"I have no idea what about, but I guess the farm will have to wait." She huffed out a breath in annoyance at the change in plans.

Sandy frowned. "Anna, about the mayor . . ."

"Yes?" She'd never seen the typically chatty woman at a loss for words. "What is it?"

Sandy clasped and unclasped her hands in a nervous gesture before clearing her throat. "She can be . . . difficult. Ever since she was elected, the society has been at odds with her. I'm afraid we've had little luck getting her to see things from our point of view. Several times, we've proposed a preservation project only for her to shoot it down."

Anna nodded. She'd known the mayor was not a fan of historic preservation. Her remarks at their first meeting had made that plain. "You're worried she'll do the same with the Cooper project."

Sandy smiled softly. "Perhaps you'll have better luck with her than we have."

She had little confidence in that, but she returned the older woman's smile, not wanting to worry her. "Let's hope so."

Rising, Sandy noted, "At least Town Hall will be a change of scenery. Get you out of this room."

When she winked, Anna chuckled. "Yes, it will."

Leave it to Sandy to find the bright side of things.

* * * *

Anna

Anna parked in front of Town Hall, realizing she hadn't been there since her first day on the job.

So much has happened since then.

She still couldn't believe someone had deliberately damaged her tire. With everything that had been going on with Richard, she'd thought little of it, but being back at the crime scene stirred up the worry brewing in her gut over what the mayor might want with her.

You won't find out sitting in your car.

As the thought made her stomach tense, she pressed a hand there to ease it and stared at the glass-fronted building. It had to feel like a greenhouse. And it was only June, not even the hottest part of summer yet. Cooling the giant ugly box must be a waste of energy, not to mention taxpayer dollars. If the mayor wanted to add more buildings like this to Rolling Brook, Anna had a long battle ahead of her.

She sighed. Thinking about things like that would add to her stress level. She shook herself and headed for the building. Nerves danced along her skin at what she was walking into. She clutched the strap of her work bag and hoped whatever the mayor wanted wouldn't be at odds with the society's plans for the town.

Blowing out a breath, she approached the reception desk outside the mayor's office. "Good afternoon. I'm here to see the mayor."

The young blonde behind the desk looked up; the abrupt end of her nails tapping on the keyboard made Anna aware of how quiet it was.

"Anna Hendricks?"

She nodded. The silence piled on her nerves, and she spoke to break it, "Yes."

The young receptionist waved to a chair across the room. "You can have a seat. I'll let the mayor know you're here."

"Thanks." She sat in the stiff plastic chair and fiddled

with her necklace as she gazed around the room.

The walls were painted a light cream, and the carpet was a braided Berber mixed with light brown in the same cream shade. A few paintings in a similar palette hung on the walls. The whole aesthetic was very neutral and, in her opinion, very uninspiring.

She shifted in her seat, her leg clinging to the plastic of the chair. It was clear and modern, a near match to the glass windows making up the façade of the building. The chair was as uncomfortable as the walls were boring, and Anna hoped she wouldn't be waiting long.

She pulled out her phone to pass the time and noticed a text message from a number she didn't recognize. Opening it, she frowned.

The message was from Richard, but she hadn't given him her number.

It's Richard. Now you have my number for when you're ready to deal. Good luck with the mayor ;)

How had he known she'd gone to see the mayor? Had he stopped by the historical society after she left? That would make sense.

I bet Sandy told him where I was.

Sighing, she closed the message and turned her phone off. Richard wasn't giving up. She wondered if Luther had talked to him yet. Maybe she should ask him—

"Miss Hendricks." Anna looked up when she heard her name. The receptionist held the mayor's door open. "She's ready for you now."

When she rose, thoughts of Luther fled as the nerves seized her again. She swallowed, her stomach churning in anxiety over what the mayor might want. Steeling against it, she took a deep breath, shook her hair back, and entered Mayor Landstrom's office.

"Anna, so nice to see you again." The mayor gestured at the cream-colored club chairs in front of her desk. "Please, have a seat."

The color scheme continued in the mayor's office. Trying not to laugh at it, Anna settled in the offered seat. While waiting for the mayor to continue, she took in the woman's glass waterfall desk, the light brown cabinets behind it, and the neutral-colored contemporary artwork on the walls. The mayor had a particular style she preferred—modern with clean lines and minimal color.

Mayor Landstrom cleared her throat, and Anna glanced back at her. "You wanted to see me?"

She noted the mayor's style extended to her wardrobe because she wore a cream suit with a white blouse. She'd styled her light brown hair meticulously, and the sole pop of color was in the turquoise gem at her throat.

The mayor's face remained calm, but Anna detected a note of irritation in the twitch of the woman's eye. Mayor Landstrom didn't seem thrilled with her lack of interest.

"Yes, dear. I understand you've come up with a proposal for the Cooper farm, but I'm here to tell you there's already a plan in the works for that property."

Anna's stomach dropped. "Oh? This is news to me. What are those plans, may I ask?" She struggled to keep her voice pleasant when she felt like screaming in frustration.

The mayor's saccharine smile grated on her nerves. "It's going to be developed, but more than that . . . I can't tell you at this time."

Oh really? Not if I can help it!

"That's interesting, Mayor Landstrom because the historical preservation society owns the property. And, as its director, I *can* tell you we have no plans to turn it into a development."

The woman's lips flattened, and her eyes hardened as she stared Anna down. After several seconds, when it was clear she refused to concede, the mayor changed tactics, pasting another fake smile on her face.

"Now, Anna. I'm sure you know the town needs more housing." She steepled her fingers on her desk and leaned forward. "That property is a prime location and a real estate developer out of Chicago is interested in it. Surely, you can understand the town will prefer added living spaces over saving a farm that is no longer being worked or even *lived* on?"

She wanted to snarl at the woman, but there was some truth in her words. They added fuel to her fears that the town wouldn't like her plans for the farm.

Taking a steadying breath, she gathered her courage and spoke. "I don't want to just 'save' the farm, Mayor. My plans for the property will turn it into an asset the town lacks."

"Unless that 'asset' includes rental housing, I think you'll have a hard time outselling the development plan." The mayor folded her hands and shrugged with a smile as though she purely pointed out the obvious.

Anna knew how to be diplomatic, how to smile and nod, and how to agree without really agreeing, but years of training from growing up in the spotlight abandoned her now. Anger over the mayor, thinking she could railroad anyone with an agenda that differed from hers, set her teeth on edge. She clenched her fists, and her nails bit into her palms.

"I suppose it will be up to the town."

Mayor Landstrom chuckled. "You have such zeal! I could use a young woman like you on my team. Surely, coming from a big city, you know the only way to keep this town alive is to allow it to grow." She rose, came around her desk, and perched on the front of it as though they were merely friends having a chat.

Her relaxed posture wasn't fooling Anna. The whole 'you and I are the same' approach was not about to work on her. "Growth is necessary, but it doesn't have to come at the cost of historic structures."

"Oh, but think of the costs associated with preserving those structures. It's less of a strain on the town to tear down and start fresh."

Anna's pulse sped, and adrenaline surged through her veins as the topic heated her ire. "That's actually a misconception. Studies have sho—"

"We could debate this all day, I'm sure, but I have another appointment."

She didn't appreciate being cut off, but she knew it meant the mayor was afraid she'd lose the argument.

Mayor Landstrom stood, and she followed suit. As she

turned to go, the mayor sighed. "Anna, it pays to have friends in this business, and I'd hate for you to burn bridges so soon."

Her hackles rose as she studied the mayor's face. The woman looked genuinely concerned, but Anna couldn't tell if it wasn't simply an act. "I'll keep that in mind."

The woman smiled, but it didn't reach her eyes. "You do that."

She was almost at the door when the mayor stopped her again.

"Oh, and Anna?"

Turning back, she asked, "Yes?"

The mayor's smile was genuine this time, but there was an edge to it. "Don't forget you're on the Development Review Committee."

She nodded, but inwardly, she winced. *Nice shot, Mayor.*

She hadn't forgotten about being stuck on a committee she wanted no part in. She left the office feeling like she'd walked into a trap. If the mayor was bringing up the committee now, it meant she had a reason to, and Anna was sure it was a reason she wouldn't like.

CHAPTER 13

Luther

Luther stopped in his tracks. He'd been thinking of Anna, and there she was, walking right toward him as if he'd conjured her with his thoughts. Her chocolate waves fell forward, obscuring her face as she dug through her bag. She was distracted and hadn't noticed him.

A grin spread across his lips, and his dimples appeared as she drew closer, still rummaging for something. Should he get her attention or let this play out?

He heard her mutter, "Fudgesicles," before she walked right into his chest.

"Oh! Sor—" Her head snapped up, and her face flushed. She readjusted the tortoise-shell glasses that had slid down her nose. For some reason, he found those glasses sexy as hell.

Luther chuckled. "A little distracted, huh?" He wanted to wrap his arms around her, but as they were in the middle of the mayor's reception room, he didn't stop her when she took a step back.

"What are you doing here?"

"I was going to ask you the same thing."

Her brow wrinkled before she looked over her shoulder at the mayor's door. "Mayor Landstrom wanted to see me."

"Everything okay?"

She visibly shook herself, and the worry cleared from her eyes. "Yes. We were discussing a project I'm working on. But why are you here? Did the mayor request to see you, too?"

"No, I asked to see *her*," he paused, his instinct not to show his hand, but Anna had a right to know. "I'm here about getting the footage from the day of the meeting. To see if I can catch whoever damaged your tire."

"Oh." When the worry returned to her face, he questioned whether he should've told her. "Did you talk to Richard?"

Running a hand through his spiky hair, he sighed. "Yeah, but I'm not sure he got the message. Has he bothered you again?"

She bit her lip as though she was hesitating to tell him something. If anxiety over Cartwright wasn't swimming in his gut, he'd have been fantasizing about biting that lip himself. He wanted another taste of her, but more than that, he wanted to know she was safe.

Finally, she released her lip and nodded. Going back to her bag, she pulled out her phone and handed it to him after turning it on. "He sent me this, but I don't know how he got my number."

Luther's hand tightened around the phone as he read the message.

Dammit!

He needed some dirt on this bastard, something he could use to hold him.

"Luther?"

His jaw started to hurt. He'd clenched it hard enough he was in danger of cracking teeth. Taking a deep breath, he pushed away the rage and returned the phone to her.

"Cartwright probably got it from your personnel file. I'm guessing those are on some shared drive you all use?" He was impressed with the evenness of his voice when his throat felt like it was closing up at the acknowledgment that his fears had come true.

Anna blinked. "They are." She swallowed, and the pulse in her throat jumped. "At least the address in the file for me is the bed and breakfast, and I'll be moving out next weekend."

He smiled as some of the fear eased. He wanted her in his building. If she was close, he could protect her. "Want some help moving in?"

She smiled, and her eyes danced. "Yes, actually."

"What's that look about? Do you have a bunch of heavy furniture or something?"

Her smile turned mischievous. "Or something. If you have any friends willing to help, I'll pay in food and wine."

He laughed. "Make it pizza and beer, and you've got a deal."

She held out her hand. "Done."

Grinning, he reached for it, but he didn't shake it.

Instead, he clasped her tiny palm, lifting it to his lips for a kiss. At her sharp intake of breath, his blood heated in response. Releasing her hand, he leaned down to whisper in her ear. "See you soon, Anna Hendricks."

She gave a slight nod, then hurried away. He breathed in deeply, savoring the scent she'd left behind.

"Officer Monroe?"

At the sound of his name, he turned. "Yeah?"

The blonde receptionist was staring at him with unabashed interest. She licked her lips, adding, "The mayor will see you now."

He ignored her look. He wanted only one woman looking at him like that, and this blonde wasn't it. That fact aside, he needed to turn on the charm for the mayor if he had any hope of getting the security footage.

Giving the receptionist a curt "Thanks," he entered the mayor's office.

* * * *

Luther

It was five o'clock the following Monday when Luther finally received the security footage from Town Hall, and he had no plans of leaving until he'd watched it. The agency that stored the data had refused to give it to him without a warrant, and he'd needed the mayor's approval to submit a request for one. His conversation with the woman the Friday before had gone smoothly, but only after he'd mentioned that Miss Hendricks's car had been the target of the vandalism.

He wasn't sure what interest the mayor had in Anna, but it set his Spidey senses on alert.

He'd heard nothing else from Anna about Cartwright, and he hoped it was because the man hadn't bothered her. His inability to act on that situation had left him tossing and turning in frustration, so much so that he'd gotten up for a run in the middle of the night. The exercise had tired him enough to allow him to sleep, but he'd woken impatient and on edge the next morning.

For some reason, Anna attracted trouble like flies to honey. He'd have one less thing to worry about if he found the vandal. Thankfully, he'd gotten the footage from the day of the meeting, so he could make that happen.

Thinking about the Suspicious Activity Reports, Luther shook his head. He could use a break in her case with the way his other investigation was headed. When it came to tracing the reports back, he was dealing with a tangled web. He was managing to unravel it, but it was slow going—one knot at a time.

The vandalism was straightforward in comparison. Pouring out a handful of Skittles, he tossed them in his mouth as he searched the videos. There were several camera angles, and he needed the one with a clear view of her car.

When he landed on it, he stopped, taking a calming breath before letting the footage play. At least he had a relatively narrow time window to go through.

He saw her pull up and exit her car in a rush. She high-tailed it for the building as if she were running late. He didn't mind because watching her backside bounce as she scurried off was a nice perk. He downed another handful of candy as the video continued to play.

Several people came and went over the next hour, but none of them ventured near her car. On a yawn, he paused the video and rose in search of caffeine. A coffee pot perched on the counter along the far wall of the bullpen, and he headed for it.

Reaching it, he lifted the pot and eyed the dark sludge that was left. Shrugging, he poured it out into a mug and took a sip. The coffee had gone cold and had the distinct taste of charcoal after being on the burner for too long. He frowned and took another sip. At least it was caffeine. Ignoring the rebellion his taste buds were raging, he carried the coffee back to his desk.

He sat down and pressed play again, knowing he had to be getting close to the time of the slashing. When Cartwright exited the building, Luther sat up straighter.

Let's see if your original story pans out.

He clutched the coffee mug as he watched Cartwright walk across the parking lot. "Where are you going?" he muttered the question aloud. But as he continued to watch, he knew.

The truth slammed into Luther's gut, and he almost dropped his half-finished mug. With fear for Anna's safety swamping him, he broke out in a cold sweat. After setting the coffee down with a hand that shook, he grabbed his keys and ran for the door.

CHAPTER 14

Luther

By the time Luther pulled up in front of Cartwright's home, he'd calmed down enough that fear was no longer choking him. He'd pushed it down until it formed a rock in his stomach, leaving his head clear for the task at hand. The surveillance video had given him the dirt he needed to arrest Cartwright. If the man were in jail, he wouldn't be able to get to Anna. Bail was likely, but the advantage of bringing the bastard in tonight was he wouldn't get a chance at it until the next day at the earliest.

The thought of Cartwright spending an uncomfortable night in a cell eased the tension in his muscles.

Anna would be safe.

Cracking his neck from side to side, he took a deep breath and exited his vehicle. He was ready for this. Not that he expected Cartwright to resist, but he'd be happy to respond with force if necessary.

A slow grin stretched across his face, thinking of the

possibility. After a few moments of relishing his fist connecting with the asshole's face, Luther shook the image from his mind and climbed the steps to the man's door.

Knocking loudly, he waited for a response, his fingers tapping an impatient rhythm on his belt holster.

It didn't take long for Cartwright to appear. The man opened the door and scowled. "Visiting again so soon?"

He kept his expression stoic. "Richard Cartwright, you're under arrest for criminal damage to property."

Cartwright's face turned a dark shade of maroon. "What? This is unbelievable! I didn't touch her vehicle!" His voice rose with each statement.

That's a lie.

"Step outside. Now." He ignored Cartwright's rant and pulled the cuffs off the clip at his waist. "And you might want to stop talking before you incriminate yourself further."

The color that had flooded Cartwright's face leached away. "I want a lawyer."

He couldn't contain his smile. "You'll get one . . . eventually."

The man's eyes widened, and his mouth shut. Without another word, he did as Luther asked.

When Cartwright was on the stoop, he turned him around. "Put your feet together and your hands behind your back."

Cartwright's shoulders drooped, and he complied. Luther cuffed him and began reciting the Miranda Warning as he led the sleazebag to his cruiser. When they reached it, he opened the back door and shoved a subdued

Cartwright in.

Sighing, disappointed that the bastard hadn't given him any resistance, Luther headed for the station.

* * * *

Anna

Anna was in the bath when she heard knocking at her door. Her eyes flew open at the sound, and she jumped up, sloshing water as she went.

Crud!

In a tizzy, she grabbed for the satin robe hanging on the back of the door. When she'd covered herself, she wrenched the bathroom door open. Rushing to her room door, she tripped over the heels lying discarded on the floor and landed in a sprawl.

Fishsticks!

She stood up and examined her right knee; it was already turning colors. Grumbling at herself for being so careless, she opened her door with a scowl.

"Yes?" When she saw it was Luther, she blushed and pulled the robe tighter around her throat.

His eyes burned hot for a moment as he took her in, but then he blinked, and they were a calm silver. Clearing his throat, he asked, "Can I come in?"

"Oh, um, sure." She stepped back and waved him inside.

She became very aware of the fact she was wearing nothing but a thin robe and regretted not getting fully dressed before answering the door. The sight of him in his uniform had heat pooling between her legs, and she clenched her thighs together against the sensation. Her stomach was in knots from the mix of dread and anticipation that hit her whenever he was near. Ever since their second kiss, fissures had formed in her defensive walls. What would she do when those cracks caused the walls to crumble?

He turned around and caught her staring. She blushed and looked away, embarrassed she'd been ogling the muscles in his back, which were visible against the white of his uniform shirt.

Mmm, Officer Yummy.

Shaking herself, she closed the door to her room, then asked, "What's this about?"

He looked at her but quickly averted his gaze. "I arrested Cartwright."

She blew out a breath in surprise. "What happened?" And why wouldn't he look at her? He kept glancing around the room instead.

She took a step toward him, and he finally met her gaze. The skin around his eyes was tight and pinched as if he were in pain.

"Did he hurt you? Are you all right?" Worry that Luther had been injured surged through her, and she advanced on him, determined to look for wounds.

"I'm fine." He held up his hands and backed away from her.

"Then what's wrong?" He was unusually distant, and for some reason, it was causing the knots in her belly to rise and tighten around her chest.

"What? Nothing's wrong. I just . . ." His eyes dipped before coming back to hers. He rubbed the back of his neck, then asked in a strained voice, "Would you want to put on some clothes?"

Her eyes widened at his comment, and she wasn't sure how to respond.

Before she had a chance to think about it, Luther shook his head. "Never mind," he paused and took a breath. "Anna, Cartwright was the one who slashed your tire. He's in custody, but he'll likely make bail tomorrow."

"Oh." She expected to feel relieved that she knew who the tire slasher was, but finding out it was Richard hit her like an icy wave.

How had she been so blind? Her thoughts swirled as her mind replayed each exchange with him. How had she missed the lies?

"Are you okay? You've gone really pale."

She blinked at Luther's voice and focused on his face. He'd taken a step toward her, and concern shone in his eyes. "What?"

"I asked if you're okay." He reached for her and brushed a hand across her cold cheek. "Look, even if Cartwright gets out on bail, he'll be ordered to stay away from you."

Her thoughts hadn't gotten that far. Now, images of Richard being let off and coming after her flooded her mind with fear. Her pulse pounded in her ears so loudly when she spoke, she wasn't aware it was barely above a whisper. "What if he doesn't?"

He squeezed one of the arms she'd hugged around herself. "He will. It'll be a condition of his bond, and if he violates it, I'll take him back to jail."

She didn't trust her voice, so she nodded. Luther's touch didn't even penetrate the scattered jumble of her thoughts. She tried to understand how this would affect her work. Would Richard get fired? How soon could the county hire someone to take his place?

Her nose scrunched up, and her forehead wrinkled. What about all the projects he'd been doing for the society? Would they get lost in the shuffle?

What am I going to tell the ladies?

At that, her heart lodged itself in her throat. Especially Dorothy, who had a soft spot for him. *Fudge!* This was a mess.

Groaning, she grabbed her head, bunching up the hair on either side of her face.

While all of that jumbled around in her skull, she hadn't thought to ask the most important question. When it smacked her between the eyes, she gasped and dropped her hands, her previous worries stuttering to a halt.

"Why? Why is he doing this?" With her eyes, Anna implored Luther to tell her the answer, to help her make sense of this unbelievable situation.

He gripped her shoulders, and when she looked into his eyes, the fear seizing her lungs loosened, allowing her to breathe easier. She wasn't alone in this.

"It doesn't matter why, Anna. What matters is we put a stop to it." His voice softened, and he cupped her cheek. "I won't let him hurt you."

She searched Luther's face. Could she trust him?

After she'd missed the signs with Richard, she wasn't

sure she trusted herself. It was apparent her judgment needed some work.

Shaking out of his hold, she stepped away from him, shivering at the loss of warmth. Ignoring it, she pulled the robe tighter around her. "Thank you for letting me know."

"Of course. Anna . . ."

She tensed, afraid of what he might say and how she might respond.

When she continued to avoid looking at him, she heard him sigh. "If you need anything, don't hesitate to ask."

She nodded, then opened the door to her room. "Goodnight."

He lingered, but she couldn't read his expression through the tears swimming in her eyes. She blinked rapidly, trying to clear them, but that only caused one of them to spill over.

He wiped the moisture away with his thumb, making the drops fall even faster. "Anna, I—" He cursed and pulled her into his arms.

In his embrace, her control splintered. Her emotions broke through the dam she used to contain them and threatened to overwhelm her. She was shaky and light-headed, even though her pulse raced and her skin heated. Her body was as confused as her brain, and she didn't know how to react as she cried her eyes out in Luther's arms.

He stroked her back in soothing circles, and it felt too good. She wanted to trust him, to ignore the possibility she could be wrong, but she didn't think she was strong enough to face the consequences if she wasn't.

The tears had stopped, and it was time to let him go. A heaviness settled in her stomach with the thought.

He pulled back first and tilted her chin up. His eyes liquid smoke as he asked, "Do you want me to stay?"

Her heart screamed yes, but Anna didn't trust it. Her mind insisted on thrusting images of Dan's betrayal at her, and she couldn't go through that again.

He must have seen the answer on her face because his eyes shuttered, the fire in them extinguished. "Goodnight, Anna."

She couldn't speak, so she merely watched him walk away. A part of her screamed to stop him, but she ignored it and closed the door.

CHAPTER 15

Luther

Anna was naked on his bed, her arms handcuffed to the bedpost. Luther's cock pulsed as he grinned down at her supple frame. Her curves might be subtle, but there was no denying her body's femininity. She shifted, the motion making her small, firm breasts bounce, and he stared, mesmerized. His eyes soaked up her beauty. Her long brown hair tangled around her shoulders, and her caramel eyes glowed up at him as he memorized every dip and rise. He couldn't believe he finally had her right where he wanted her.

"I want to touch you," she pouted, her luscious strawberry lip poking out as she struggled against the cuffs.

He chuckled. "You'll get your turn." Bending down, he nipped her pouty lip before sucking it into his mouth. She sighed, and her sweet candy flavor flooded his senses. He was going to taste every inch of her, lick every curve, but first, he had something else in mind.

Releasing her mouth, he grabbed the bag of Skittles off his nightstand. He poured out a handful and then started to place them all over her body.

"That tickles." She squirmed, and a few fell off.

"Don't move, Shortcake."

"But—"

Smiling, he made his voice stern as he said, "It's against the law."

"Okay, Officer Hottie." She giggled, and a few more slid off.

He changed tactics and licked her skin before placing the Skittles on, hoping the moisture would help them adhere. It did.

He started tasting when he had enough of the candy where he wanted it. Her legs were a buffet of grape and orange, and he sampled his way up before moving on to her breasts. They were a feast of lemon and lime. He lingered there, enjoying the taste of citrus and the mewling coming from Anna at the touch of his tongue on her nipples. Strawberry, his favorite flavor, he'd saved for last.

He set a red Skittle between her breasts and tilted his head toward it. With a deep breath, he began to blow it down her chest.

She gasped when the warm air washed over her, and he drew in another lungful. When he blew the candy further south, she groaned. The sound sent a surge of pleasure coursing through him, and he kept blowing until the Skittle got stuck in her belly button.

Undeterred, he captured it with his tongue, then

lavished his attention on that sensitive area.

She started to buck beneath him, but he allowed it. He only needed one more Skittle. Leaving her navel, he placed another red one below it and started to blow. she whimpered when the candy landed right where he wanted it—between her legs.

Grinning up at her, he bent his head to retrieve the strawberry Skittle just as a knock sounded at the door.

Dammit!

"Is that the door?" Her voice was breathy with pleasure.

He glanced toward it. "Nope." He had no intention of answering it.

But as he turned his gaze back to Anna, his vision clouded, and a roaring sounded in his ears.

"Luther!"

He shot awake in his bed, then fell back with a growl when he grasped it had all been a dream. Well, not *all* a dream. He adjusted himself with a grunt. His physical response was very real.

"Luther!"

As his brain cleared, he realized the banging on his door wasn't part of the dream, and someone was calling his name.

Shit!

He scrambled out of bed and threw on the first clothes he saw—gym shorts and a T-shirt.

"Coming!" he called in a voice rough from sleep as he headed for the front door.

Though not in the way I'd like.

When he opened it, his hard-on had subsided—mostly.

"Morning!" Cassie's voice was far too cheery for how crummy he felt.

What the hell time was it anyway?

"Cass. Everything okay? Why are you pounding on my door so early in the morning?"

She laughed as if he'd said something funny. "It's not early. It's eight o'clock. Anyway, I wanted to ask if you were still willing to help me move some stuff out?"

He sighed; he'd had another fifteen minutes on his alarm. Fifteen minutes would have let him finish the dream he'd been having. "Sure. When do you need help?"

She beamed. "Tonight! Shane will be here too, but with your help, it'll take no time at all."

"Great. See you tonight."

"Thanks, Luther!"

"No problem." He shut the door and leaned back against it. After the way he'd left things with Anna, sleep had eluded him much of the night, and now he would have to help Cassie move when he was already bone-tired.

He rubbed at the ache in his chest as he thought about how she'd turned him down—again. Whenever he thought he'd moved a step closer, she took a step back.

Frustrated on multiple fronts, he scrubbed his hands down his face.

Coffee and a shower. If he was going to make it through this day, that's what he needed.

* * * *

Luther

As soon as Luther stepped inside the police station, Sergeant Jameson descended on him.

"Sarg—"

"Not here," the sergeant growled as he steered Luther toward the empty lieutenant's office. The sound of whistles and jeers echoed from the bullpen.

What is going on?

His sleep-deprived brain wasn't sure why he appeared to be in trouble, but he didn't protest when the sergeant shoved him into a chair and took the seat across the desk from him.

"What the fuck, Monroe?" Sergeant Jameson's face was bright red as he glared at Luther.

"Sarge, what's wrong?"

"What do you mean, 'what's wrong'?" The sergeant's eyes narrowed to slits, and if it were possible to see steam come out of the man's ears, he would've done so. "You want to tell me why the fuck the mayor's nephew spent the night in jail?"

What the hell?

He swallowed around the lump that had formed in his throat. "Do you mean Cartwright?"

"No shit!" Sarge yelled. "What the hell were you thinking?"

He winced as Sergeant Jameson's voice boomed at him. "Damn. I didn't know."

Sarge scrubbed a hand over his face. "The captain was ready to suspend you—"

He blanched, and his heart dropped to his stomach.

"—but I talked him out of it."

Blowing out a breath in relief, Luther spoke. "Thanks, Sarge."

Sergeant Jameson frowned at him. "It wasn't a favor. I need you to keep investigating," he paused and glanced at the door. Even though it was closed, he shook his head before continuing, "The other case I've tasked you with. Got it?"

"Yes, sir."

"Good. Maybe get out of here for a while. I don't want you to cross paths with the captain right now."

"Is he out? Cartwright?"

Sarge sighed. "Yeah. He posted bail first thing this morning."

Luther scowled. "The bastard deserved a night in a cell."

"For slashing a tire?"

He shrugged, and the sergeant eyed him closely before asking, "This is about the woman, isn't it? You're gonna let a piece of ass screw up your career?"

He shot to his feet and got in Sarge's face. "Don't call her that!"

Sergeant Jameson didn't back down; in fact, he started laughing. "Fuck, Monroe. Are you in love with her?"

Luther blinked, and his anger evaporated. *Love?*

He lowered to his chair as his thoughts spun.

The sergeant rose to leave, but he clapped him on the shoulder on his way out the door. "Welcome to the club. Now get the hell out of here."

With a nod, he stood. He left the lieutenant's office to more calls and whistles thrown in his direction as he waded through the bullpen, but they washed over him in a daze. He was still processing what Sergeant Jameson had said.

Am I in love with Anna?

* * * *

Luther

Luther parked at the far end of the lot in front of the Shoppes at Rolling Brook. He'd headed there after Sarge had kicked him out of the station. The same as it had been a couple of weeks before when he'd first come to investigate the report of suspicious activity, the parking lot was nearly empty. He counted seven other cars—not enough to keep this place afloat . . . *if* the business conducted here was legitimate.

He was close to finding the truth about that. Drumming his fingers on the steering wheel, he stared at the buildings' faux facades. Several remained empty despite the records he'd found claiming they were rented out. The whole thing was a house of cards, and he was worried about the fallout when it came crashing down. Not that he was ready to demolish it . . . but he *was* getting closer.

It was clear to him the Shoppes were a front organization for money laundering. The pizzeria had to be a shell company, and it was likely the other businesses here were, too. But what he was still working on was whose money they were laundering. He ran a hand down his face in frustration. And he didn't know who was involved from town.

Someone in the department had made an effort to bury

the Suspicious Activity Reports. He knew it wasn't Sergeant Jameson, but that's where his confidence ended when it came to the rest of the men and women he worked with. His gut told him Haines was involved, but if that was the case, he didn't want to tip his hand by asking questions . . . yet.

Letting out a heavy sigh, Luther started his cruiser. He wasn't going to find the answers he needed staring at empty buildings. Not about this investigation or the question Sarge had asked him that morning. He didn't have an answer in either case.

Or did he?

Luther's chest tightened at the thought. The last girl he'd loved had thrown his heart away, and he wasn't sure he was ready to offer it up for the same kind of treatment. After he'd graduated from the police academy, he'd come home prepared to propose to his high school sweetheart only to find she'd already moved on . . . and into bed with another guy.

He rubbed at his chest as the pain of the memory coursed through him. He wasn't ready for the "L" word. At least not the one involving his heart. But he *was* looking forward to seeing Anna again. With a grin, he gunned it out of the parking lot.

CHAPTER 16

Anna

Anna bit into a carrot and watched Luther and Shane grimace under the weight of the latest crate they'd hauled up the stairs to her apartment. There were a lot of grunts and curse words involved, so it had to be one of the heavier ones. When she'd left D.C., she'd had all her belongings packed and stored in a container. Once she'd agreed to take over Cassie's rental, she'd contacted the storage company and set up the delivery. After working for the last two hours, the four of them had nearly emptied it.

Smiling when Luther and Shane set the crate down exactly where she'd instructed them to, she reached for a cucumber slice from the crudités she'd thrown together to go with the pizza and beer she'd promised.

Cassie sat on a box next to her, nibbling on a slice of pepperoni. They'd made themselves comfortable as soon as the pizza showed up, but the men were determined to finish moving the heavy stuff in before they enjoyed any of it.

"I feel a little guilty we're not helping," she confessed to Cassie, but she wasn't only feeling guilty about that.

Despite how often she reminded herself not to get tangled up with Luther, she couldn't stop looking at him. He wore a tank top that left his arms bare, and they were corded with muscles. Earlier, he'd lifted up his shirt to wipe at the sweat on his forehead, and she'd gotten a peek at the six-pack beneath. Her pulse jumped whenever she thought about what he looked like with his shirt off.

Cassie shook her head, and the motion made her blonde hair swing against her shoulders, drawing Anna's attention away from Luther's muscles. She focused on the woman she was starting to call a friend.

After Cassie swallowed the bite of pizza she'd been working on, she spoke, "Don't feel guilty. We'd just be in the way right now." She smiled, and her blue eyes twinkled. "Besides, we offered them some. They'll take a break when they're ready."

Anna returned the smile. The tension she carried in her shoulders loosened in Cassie's company. She was grateful the blonde had come with Shane after Luther had roped him into helping move her stuff in. He'd told her it was quid pro quo after he'd helped Cassie move her things *out* a few days before.

"All of you must be tired after moving twice in the same week."

Cassie chuckled. "I don't know about them, but I'm too excited to be tired. I can't believe I'm living with Shane now. It's a big step for us." She stared at Shane's back as he bent over to shove a box out of the walkway.

When he turned around, Anna saw his shaggy black hair had matted to his forehead from sweat, but it didn't detract from his looks. He was handsome in a rugged sort of way, and his light green eyes lit up whenever they landed on Cassie.

She noticed the woman's cheeks turn pink under Shane's scrutiny. Placing her hand over Cassie's, she gave it a quick squeeze. "You two seem happy together."

Cassie nodded as Luther and Shane disappeared through the front door. "I don't have the best track record, which Luther can attest to, but with Shane . . ." Her eyes got a faraway look before she blinked and focused on Anna. "I knew things would be different, you know?"

At Cassie's comment, she struggled to keep her smile in place. Why would Luther know about her relationship history? Had they been a couple?

Anna cleared her throat around the lump that had lodged itself there. "You and Luther are close?"

"Yes. We've been like brother and sister since kindergarten. Growing up, people always thought we were siblings since our coloring is so similar." She chuckled. "We fought like we were. But he's always been there for me. And then when his dad passed . . ." She took a deep breath. "I'd lost my mom a few years before, so I understood what he was going through."

"I'm sorry, Cassie." She didn't know what else to say. She wasn't close with her parents these days, but she couldn't imagine what it would be like to lose them as a child.

"Thanks. It was a long time ago now."

She wanted to pry about Luther's past, but it wasn't any of her business. She was also enjoying Cassie's company and didn't want to stir up bad memories for her new friend.

In an attempt to lighten the mood, she stood. "I think it's happy hour. What about you?"

Cassie chuckled. "Thanks, I'll have a beer."

Her eyebrows hiked up at that. "Really? I have a rosé."

Cassie smiled but shook her head. "I'm not much of a wine drinker. The beer is fine for me."

Anna's eyes widened before she hid her shock. How anyone preferred beer over wine was beyond her, especially rosé. But knowing her duties as hostess, she offered Cassie a smile. "All right. Would you like a glass? I'm going to have to find one for the wine anyway."

"I'll drink it from the bottle. No point in making more dishes for you." The blonde stood and followed her into the kitchen to retrieve the beer from the refrigerator.

When Luther and Shane came through the front door, they'd just returned to the living room and the makeshift dining set they'd made out of crates and boxes.

They were breathing heavily, and Luther shouted with his back to her, "This is the last big item. Anna, where do you want it?"

They paused in the middle of the living room, and she rushed forward to read the label. She gestured to a spot under the window when she understood what it was. "Right there, against the wall."

Shane blew the hair out of his eyes, and Luther clenched his teeth as they attempted to lower the heavy wooden crate to the floor slowly. They were a couple of inches away from succeeding when Shane lost his grip, and it clunked against the hardwood. She winced and hoped what was inside didn't break.

"Sorry, man," Shane apologized as Luther set his end down before it fell on his fingers.

"It's okay." He flexed his digits, and she saw red marks from where he'd gripped the crate so tightly.

She frowned as she stared at his hands. Had she noticed how long his fingers were before? She wondered if they'd have more calluses after today and how different they might feel if he brushed her cheek with them . . . or other sensitive areas.

Cassie bounded over with a beer in each hand, and Anna blinked, pulling herself out of that dangerous line of thinking with a blush at the turn of her thoughts.

"Time for a break, boys!"

The blonde handed one of the beers to Shane, and Luther asked, "Hey, where's mine?"

She took a sip of the other bottle she held, then grinned. "The refrigerator."

He glared at Cassie, which made her laugh and smile at the exchange. They *were* like brother and sister.

He turned his attention to her, and the glare in his eyes had become a glint. "You owe me a drink. How about I try this one?" He reached for her wine glass and took it from her grip before she'd realized what he intended.

"Oh, but—"

Luther took a sip. "Not bad." Then he winked. "Kind of tastes like strawberries."

Her cheeks heated at the mention of strawberries, and she met his gaze. While they stared at one another, his smile faded, and his eyes ignited, sending an answering warmth coursing through her.

When he took a step toward her, the movement broke his hold, and she almost sagged in relief. She had to put some distance between them before she threw all caution to the wind.

Turning away from the hunger in his eyes, she called over her shoulder, "I'll get you a beer."

* * * *

Luther

Frowning, Luther stared after Anna as she retreated to the kitchen. She was still running away, and he didn't know why. It renewed the ache in his chest, a dull throbbing over his heart that wouldn't stop. Since his encounter with Sarge a few days ago, he'd been pondering his question.

Am I in love with Anna?

Absently, Luther took another sip of her wine. The flavor burst in his mouth, and the image of him eating strawberries off her naked body flashed in his mind. He wasn't sure about love, but he was definitely in lust. The wine tasted like her, and he was thirsty for more.

He blinked at the sound of Cassie's laughter and turned to his friends. He'd almost forgotten they were there.

"You've got it bad," Cassie smirked at him before taking another sip of her beer.

"You're one to talk." He looked pointedly at Shane before

raising an eyebrow at her.

She grinned, then noisily kissed Shane's cheek. "Sure do!"

This had all three of them laughing, but he stopped when Anna walked back in. She handed him a beer, then frowned at the wine glass he returned to her.

"You drank most of it," she pouted, and his eyes were drawn to her lips.

The bottom one poked out, and he desperately wanted to capture it with his teeth. He wasn't sure how long he stared at her mouth in silence, but the sound of Shane clearing his throat brought Luther's attention back to the room.

"We should probably get going." Shane tried to hide a grin as he tugged at Cassie's arm.

"Oh, but you didn't have any pizza!" Anna exclaimed.

He stopped edging toward the door and looked with longing at the pizza boxes the girls had set on the makeshift table. "Uh, would you mind if we took some to go?"

Luther chuckled, knowing Shane had to be starving. He'd worked up an appetite moving Anna's heavy furniture—or whatever she had in those crates—and if he hadn't focused on a different type of hunger, he would have already scarfed some pizza himself.

"Of course not!" She placed her wine glass on a box and moved to the table.

He followed and snagged a slice with sausage as she divvied up the pizza.

When she'd finished, she stood and handed one of the

boxes to Shane. "Thank you both for helping me move in."

Cassie gave her a quick hug. "You're welcome! It's been fun, Anna. I hope we can hang out again soon." She glanced at Luther and winked. "Who knows, maybe we could go on a double date."

Anna sputtered, and he had to grin as Cassie and Shane made a quick exit.

"So . . ." Luther turned his grin on Anna, whose face remained several shades of red. "What's your favorite kind of pizza?" He took a bite of his and chewed as he watched her eyes flicker in confusion before her face settled into a smile.

"Ham and pineapple."

He cringed. "Seriously?" He shook his head. "Well, thanks for not ordering *that*. You know the only people who like pineapple on their pizza are psychopaths and sadists, right?" He raised an eyebrow. "Which are you?"

She laughed loudly, and the sound of it made him smile. She was as relaxed as he'd ever seen her. "Neither. Just someone who loves sweet and savory combos."

His brain shorted at her comment about sweet and savory as the urge to watch her eat pineapple off a particular part of *his* anatomy struck.

Damn, they needed to have some fun with food.

She sat on one of the boxes she'd set by the makeshift table, and he mentally shook himself. He had to move carefully if he didn't want her pulling back from him again. Food was not a safe topic of conversation.

She bit into a slice of sausage pizza, then licked her lip to catch the little bit of sauce that ended up there.

Watching her, he nearly groaned out loud.

Look away!

Clearing his throat, he reached for another slice of pizza while asking, "So what's in all these heavy crates? They look like something you'd see delivered to a museum."

She smiled, and her eyes lit up. "Want to help me open them and find out?"

Her excitement was infectious, and he smiled in response. "Absolutely."

She pointed. "Let's start with that one."

She jumped up and headed for the crate Shane had almost dropped on his fingers.

She would *want to start with the heavy one.*

He swallowed another bite of pizza and joined her. The crate had been wrapped in plastic, but she was already removing it.

Looking at the wooden box underneath, he noticed opening it wouldn't be easy. "Um, Anna. Do you have a crowbar?"

She took a step back and frowned at the crate. "Yes, but—"

Biting her lip, she turned to survey the room, and he got lost, staring at her mouth again. He was dying to kiss her and capture that spot with his teeth.

"—it's in a box, somewhere."

He tore his eyes from her lips and glanced around her living room. It was practically full of boxes. "I don't suppose you know which one?"

She looked at him. "No clue," she said, then burst out laughing. When she managed to stop chuckling, she asked,

"Do you have one?"

He'd been smiling like an idiot at the sound of her laughter. She was truly beautiful when she laughed. It made her eyes shine and her whole face light up. He could almost see the weight she always carried slip away. "I love your laugh."

Her face sobered, and her eyes widened. "You do?"

Seeing the surprise on her face, he wondered how no one had told her that before. He took a step toward her, and when she didn't back away, he smiled. She wasn't running . . . yet. "Yeah."

Testing the waters, he pushed a strand of hair behind her ear and relished how soft it was. He wanted to put his hands in it, to feel the long brown locks drape over him as she knelt between his legs. Wanting that, wanting her, he took another step.

When he was close enough for their bodies to touch, he tilted her chin up to meet his gaze. The hunger he felt echoed in her eyes. On seeing it, his pulse raced, but he forced himself to slowly bend his head to meet her in case she changed her mind. His heartbeat pounded in his ears, but he stopped with his lips a whisper away. As their breaths mingled, she closed her eyes and leaned into him. It was all the invitation he needed.

Luther covered her lips with his own and savored her taste. It was sweet, like strawberries from the wine she'd drunk. The flavor of the rosé melded with her perfume— the same fruit-laden scent that had driven him wild since they'd met, and he got lost in it, in her.

Her lips parted, and he growled deep in his throat when

her tongue swept over his. He moved his hand from her face to fist it in her hair as he groped for control of the hunger gnawing at him to take his fill. With his other hand, he molded her shape from her hip to her face and craved the contact of her skin on his.

Not yet.

Keeping his hand gentle, he cupped her cheek, even though he wanted desperately to use it to lift her legs around his waist. As he continued to sample her, she made a whimpering sound in the back of her throat that threatened to snap his control. His pants were too tight as it was, and Anna . . . tiny and pliant Anna, making sexy noises, was hard to resist.

He broke the kiss with a groan, but he wasn't ready to let her go. He wrapped his arms around her and laid his cheek on her head.

"Yeah," he huffed out through the appetite for her squeezing his insides.

"Yes, what?" Her voice was soft, and her breath was quick as she tilted her head back to meet his gaze.

The dazed look on her face nearly crushed his resolve. He took a deep breath and looked away from those golden-brown pools so full of desire. No matter what her eyes said, he wouldn't push her. He needed her to say the words—to ask. Because he wasn't going to take her when she wasn't ready.

"Yes, I have a crowbar."

"Oh."

But good intentions only went so far. Struggling against his own need, he released her, and the ache returned to his chest.

"I'll go get it."

Not looking back at her, he walked away before he took things too far, too fast.

CHAPTER 17

Anna

"Is this furniture or décor?" Luther asked as they finished unboxing Anna's most prized possession.

"Both!" It was a bench made from architectural salvage—a testament to history as well as art. Seeing the bench again was like seeing an old friend, and Anna couldn't help running her hands along the top of it.

The back and seat were fashioned from 18th-century paneled doors made of heart pine. They'd been stripped to a honey-gold color that warmed under her hand. The arms were 19th-century wooden corbels she'd spent weeks scraping off years of chipped paint. She'd finished them in a clean, crisp white that let the eccentric Victorian details shine.

Tracing a finger along the delicate swirls, she beamed at Luther. "Isn't it gorgeous!"

The white of the arms contrasted with the black of the legs, which were made from pieces of cast iron railing posts that had been cut and welded on.

She stepped back and glanced down at it with her hands clasped together. It was missing the cushion. The funky geometric pattern in black and white would pull the stark colors of the arms and legs together. She had it in a box *somewhere.*

She surveyed the small mountain of them in her living room. She'd find it . . . eventually.

Or was it in one of the crates?

Her forehead wrinkled as she tried to remember. Each crate Luther and Shane had carried in held a preserved piece of architecture. Some were wall décor, like the antique fanlight they'd yet to unbox and the stained-glass mirror she intended to hang by her front door. Even her headboard was crafted from a salvaged archway with delicate wood carvings. She couldn't wait to unbox it. The smaller crates held items like candlesticks made from balusters, bookends that had once been wall brackets, and shelves that had served as decorative molding. Maybe she'd put it in one of those?

No, that didn't make sense. How would she open them?

Shrugging, she turned back to Luther. "I'm so glad it didn't get damaged in the move."

Or when you and Shane dropped it. She grinned at him, delighted her fears about cracks in the centuries-old lumber were unfounded.

"I'm glad it didn't damage me." She heard him mutter. "Do you know how heavy this thing is?" he asked louder.

She laughed. "No, but with dense wood and cast iron. . ." She tapped a finger to her lip in thought. "I'm guessing pretty substantial. I'm impressed you and Shane were able to carry it up two flights of stairs. I think they used a forklift when they took it out of my apartment in D.C."

His eyes narrowed at her. "You could've warned us."

"Uh-huh." She tried to hold in a laugh, but her eyes gave her away.

"Think that's funny, do you?" He advanced on her, and she took a step back.

She hit the wall when he kept coming. "What are you doing?" She side-stepped and started backing in the opposite direction, keeping him in her sight.

He turned with her, though, and his eyes promised mischief. "I'll show you funny."

She reversed into a stack of boxes and squealed as she felt herself tumbling backward over them. Before she hit the ground, Luther was there. His arms caught her and pulled her up against him.

She had to suppress a moan as her body hummed from the contact. Her arms were caught between them, so she splayed her hands over his chest. His heart stuttered at her touch, and she glanced up at him. The mischievous gleam in his eyes was gone. In its place was a pulsing need so strong it made her catch her breath.

Staring into those dark, hungry depths, she swallowed, hoping and fearing he would kiss her again.

She chewed her lip as she waited; he surprised her when he pushed her back to arm's length and then turned away.

"What do you want to open next?" He returned to the first crate they'd opened and picked up the crowbar.

The distance left her feeling cold, and she suppressed a shiver. Had she misread what she'd seen in his eyes? Her mouth twisted. It *was* possible. Her experience was limited enough to make her second-guess.

Brushing off the sting of rejection she refused to acknowledge, she cleared her throat and gestured at the next crate she saw. "How about this one?"

He walked over with the crowbar as if that charged moment never happened. "Sure."

He started to pry open the large shallow crate, and she chastised herself. They *should* just be friends. It would be for the best. Wouldn't it?

Staring mindlessly at the wooden box, she started to pick at her fingernails—an anxious habit she'd broken years before. She needed him as a friend, a shoulder to lean on, especially with the whole Richard situation.

Yes, it's for the best.

Despite what she told herself, she wasn't entirely convinced. Whenever Luther was near, her system reacted in a way that was more than friendly. Even now, as she watched the muscles in his arms bulge when he pried at the crate, her nerve endings were on full alert, and she wanted to touch him, to trace her finger along those ridges.

He caught her staring, and she looked away, blushing. *Oh, snap!*

"See something you like?" He smirked at her, and her face turned an even brighter shade of red.

What game is he playing?

At the thought, her blood cooled, and she stared him down. "Is this a game? Because I'm not in the mood to play." She wasn't about to be the butt of another joke.

The smile left his eyes, and a line marred his forehead. "What do you mean?"

"This." She waved a hand between them. "You. Flirting with me, kissing me, then pushing me away." She scowled. She wanted the truth. About all of it. "Why are you helping me?"

He eyed her closely as he set the crowbar down and walked toward her with his hands up. Like she was an animal he needed to gentle.

I'll show him gentle!

"Anna, I'm helping you because I want to."

When he would've laid his hands on her shoulders, she tensed. "Don't!" Taking a step back, she demanded, "But what do you expect in return?"

She heard him sigh and thought she saw a flicker of . . .

No. Anna told herself. It couldn't have been pain she'd seen in his eyes.

"Nothing you don't want to give."

"What?" It was her turn to look confused. She tilted her head slightly and pursed her lips. What did he mean by that—exactly?

"I like you. I enjoy flirting with you and kissing you. But if you think I'm the one pushing you away . . ." He grimaced, then shook his head. "That's the opposite of what I want."

She frowned at him as she tried to comprehend what he was saying. So . . . he did want her. But for what? "What *do* you want from me, Luther?"

He scrubbed his hands over his face, and when his eyes met hers, the tempest was brewing. It thundered in their depths, and she instinctively took a step back, afraid of what might be unleashed on her.

"I don't want anything *from* you. I just want to be with you." His chest visibly rose and fell with the force of his breaths, and his hands clenched into fists. "Why is that so hard to understand?" He threw his last question at her in a snarl.

"Because!" she yelled, her anger responding to his. "Because . . ." The words she'd been ready to hurl at him caught in her throat. *Because I don't trust you, I don't trust any man.*

Her eyes flooded, but she blinked, determined not to fall apart in front of him again. She hugged herself and turned away as she struggled to get the tears under control.

"Because what, Anna?" His voice had softened, but when he turned her to face him, a storm of anguish still stirred the silver of his eyes.

"Because how do I know it's the truth?" Her vision swirled with indecision as she whispered the question that had plagued her for so long.

He frowned, but his hand was gentle as he swept it across her cheek. "Who hurt you, baby?" he murmured.

A sob tried to escape, but she swallowed it down. She felt like she was standing on the edge of a cliff. Did she stay on solid ground where it was safe, or was she brave enough to step off and chance some broken bones? Unsure, she stared up at Luther.

The storm died down, and his eyes warmed to a pale

blue. He took a step back, giving her space to make the decision.

Should she tell him about Dan? What did she have to lose? Her pride?

No. Anna mentally winced. *My heart.*

Could she risk it again? If she let Luther breach her walls, he'd be able to hurt her.

Staring into his eyes, she knew the pain of his betrayal would be much worse than Dan's. But perhaps the possibility of pain was better than submitting to a life alone. She'd been condemning herself to a lonely existence by keeping secrets.

It was time to drop her walls and see what happened because if she never risked her heart again, she might be safe from the pain of having it broken, but she'd never have a chance to mend it. And she wanted to be whole.

She took a deep breath, steeling herself to reveal her awful past relationship. "His name was Dan."

* * * *

Luther

Luther ran a hand through Anna's hair as he thought about what she'd told him. They'd moved to the bench, and he sat with her in his arms.

Dan was an asshole, and he wished he could go back in time to kick the frat boy's ass for what he did to Anna. Picturing it, his hand stilled, and his jaw clenched.

She shifted and sighed softly. Looking down at her, he forced himself to relax. His anger was useless and not what she needed right now. No matter how much Dan's actions made Luther want to find and pound on him.

I mean, what kind of guy hurts a woman that way?

Dan spent weeks lying to her so he could steal her virginity to win a bet. Luther didn't mind playing games, but only when the woman knew she was a player. What Dan did to Anna was just cruel.

No wonder she'd been so quick to shut him down. He couldn't change her past, but he could show her a better future. She deserved that and much more.

Bending to kiss her head, he breathed in her fruity scent. The smell had visions of his dream replaying in his head, and he wondered how long until she'd be ready for something like that.

He sighed inwardly. At least now he knew why she'd been so conflicted when it came to him. It had been hard for her to open up, to tell him something that had caused her so much pain, but he was happy she'd trusted him with it instead of pushing him away again.

He leaned his head back against the wall and closed his eyes. She felt so right in his arms. Too right.

This was more than lust . . . he was falling for her. As he acknowledged it, his heart skipped a beat. Was he ready to gamble it a second time? Did he have a choice?

She shifted again, and his arms automatically tightened. *No.* He'd already made the choice.

She chuckled softly. "We should probably open the rest of the crates."

"Mmm, what crates?" Wanting a few more minutes with her, he stroked a hand down her back. It tangled in her long hair, and he couldn't help the image that followed. He wanted her in his bed, his fingers wrapped in her hair as he entered her. But wanting that, he had to proceed with caution.

He was still a little shocked she hadn't been with anyone since Dan. She was virtually untouched. The realization made his stomach knot with fear and his pulse race with excitement.

All mine.

While the thought was heady, it carried a weight, too, a responsibility that made him hesitate.

Slow. They would take things slow, and he wouldn't pressure her. In fact, she deserved a little wooing.

He opened his eyes and grinned as the thought struck him. "Anna," he waited for her to sit up and look at him before he said, "go on a date with me."

She chewed her lip, and he tried not to look at it, focusing on her eyes instead. "When?"

"Tomorrow."

She stared at him for the longest second of his life, but then her golden eyes sparkled as a smile crossed her face. "All right."

Anticipation danced along his skin, but he pushed it away for now. Giving her a quick kiss on the forehead, he stood. "Great! Let's get the rest of your stuff unpacked."

CHAPTER 18

Luther

"Oh! I didn't know this was here." Anna turned to Luther with a huge smile on her face after catching sight of the sign they just passed.

"I'm glad I could surprise you." He grinned at her before focusing on the narrow driveway that led them through a forest preserve to the living history museum.

A fur trader founded Stevenstown, one of Illinois' earliest settlements. He'd visited the historic site on a school field trip many years ago and knew it would be something she'd enjoy. He'd also figured there'd be no chance they'd run into Cartwright if they left Rolling Brook. An out-of-town trip was a safer option.

Because it was summer, the museum held reenactment programs for visitors during the day, and at night, local bands set up for concerts on the lawn in front of the main historic home.

As he drove, the morning sunshine peeked through

flowering vines and dark green leafy trees. Luther cracked his window and let the shady air fill the car. It blew several strands of Anna's hair across her face, and he chuckled, watching her scramble to pull it from her eyes.

"You need a head scarf, Shortcake," he joked.

He smiled at the image forming in his head of them cruising into the sunset in a convertible, her wearing those funky cat-eye sunglasses from the 60s with a bright scarf covering her chocolate hair.

She certainly had an Audrey Hepburn thing going with her long locks piled on top of her head in some puffy updo and the sleek black jumpsuit she had on. He figured if anyone could pull off the Hollywood look, it'd be her.

She rolled her eyes at him. "Must've left it in my basket purse."

He let out a bark of laughter at her answer and shook his head. He liked it when she got sassy with him.

His goal for their date was to help her relax and show her he wasn't playing games; he just wanted to spend time with her.

Sure, every time her big doe eyes smiled at him behind those sexy tortoise-shell glasses or her breath caught in excitement, he fought the urge to kiss her strawberry lips, but that was understandable. She was beautiful, and he had a driving need to show her what sex should be like, to erase her past experience and replace it with how much pleasure he could bring her.

The wind shifted, blowing her fruity Skittle's scent into his nose. His hand itched toward the glove compartment for the candy he had stashed there before he stopped himself. Lately, he couldn't eat them without remembering his dream where he'd licked them off her skin.

Pressure built below his waist, and he shifted in his seat. They'd get there, but she needed time. He wanted her trust, not just her body. He was willing to do whatever it took to earn it because what he'd get when he gained it would be worth it.

Watching her eyes light up when the tan stone of the mid-nineteenth-century buildings came into view, he released a pent-up breath and pulled into a parking spot. His chest felt alternately too big and too tight.

Something told him he was dangling over a precipice on a rope that was slowly unraveling. He might not be leaping into love, but he wasn't trying to keep the rope from snapping, either.

* * * *

Anna

As a first date went, Luther was already winning in her book. There were few things Anna loved more than history and museums.

The Stevenstown settlement dated from the mid-1800s and showcased the original trading post of the area, a woodworker's shop turned school, and the home of the original frontiersman. They toured it all—at her insistence.

He'd been a great sport, though, smiling as she dragged him from exhibit to exhibit. Native Americans settled in the area first, and archaeological sites dotted the forest preserve surrounding the homesite. One was open for visitors, and while she'd taken a peek at the dig, she'd never cared much for playing in the dirt. The history they unearthed thrilled her, but she was happy to see it after the fact on display in a museum.

Luther caught the wrinkling of her nose as they stood over the roped-off site and smirked. "Never wanted to be Indiana Jones, I take it?"

She was getting used to his teasing; it didn't fill her with embarrassment or anger. Instead, she chuckled and shrugged. "No. I always imagined I'd be the curator in those stories. Helping with research but letting someone else get their hands dirty."

He smiled at her and pushed her falling glasses up her nose before tapping her on the end of it. "I can picture that perfectly."

He'd stepped closer with the movement, and his silver-blue eyes dropped to her lips. When they met hers again, they glowed with something that made her heart flutter. The sensation was wholly uncomfortable.

She swallowed over the nerves, tightening her throat. "So, what's next?"

He grinned, the heat in his gaze slipping away. "It's a surprise."

She exhaled in relief even though she was always wary of surprises. As much as she enjoyed being with him, she was still nervous about messing it up. Her lack of experience with dating kept nudging her insecurities.

She wasn't sure what else he had in store for the day or if it could top what they'd already done. He'd arranged the perfect date activity for her, and his thoughtfulness was wearing down her defenses.

She stared at their joined hands as he tugged her back to the main entrance and couldn't help but admire the veins running over the back of his palm. The excitement his touch brought was there, but more than that, she felt comfortable—safe.

It made her chew her lip. They were more than halfway through the day, and she never wanted it to end. Unless . . . she snuck a glance at him under her lashes. Would he kiss her when it did?

She wanted him to, which scared her so much that she forced her mind on something else.

Though the living history displays they'd visited had been for her enjoyment, some of the exhibits she'd seen would work well in Rolling Brook. They gave her ideas for sprucing up the historical society's downstairs museum.

Planning it out kept her thoughts busy until he stopped them in front of the stone trading post building. She sighed when she noticed the time. The museum closed in thirty minutes.

She squeezed his hand and said, "I suppose we have to leave soon."

He squeezed back, leaned in, and whispered in her ear, "Nope."

His breath fanning over her sensitive skin sent a shiver through her body that heated her from the inside out. Her cheeks flamed when he pulled back to look at her. She hated how obvious her reaction to him was.

Clearing her throat, she arched a brow. "What are we doing, then, if the museum closes?"

He pointed at a wooden stage she hadn't noticed before. "How 'bout dinner and a concert?"

As what he said sunk in, a giddy feeling washed over her at the date not being over. "Really?" she asked with a tentative smile.

"Time to gather provisions," he answered with a wink.

Pulling her in front of him, he laid his hands on her shoulders and gave her a nudge. "Follow the scent of funnel cake."

A food truck had arrived and set up on the opposite side of the stage. Wafting in their direction, she breathed in the sweet, fried temptation of the classic fair treat. But she hoped they were having more for dinner than funnel cake.

By the time they'd ordered hot dogs, curly fries, and a funnel cake with all the toppings, the band had set up. Music floated on the cool evening air in soft notes mixed with rapid beats.

Luther led her to a spot halfway to the stage where a pale blue blanket covered the springy grass. On top of it, a bottle of the same wine she'd been drinking when he'd helped her move in sat in a basket filled with ice.

She caught his gaze. "Is this ours?"

He smiled and nodded. Lowering to take a seat on the blanket, he set his plates down and gestured for her to do the same.

Chewing her lip in thought, Anna slowly sank beside him and whispered, "Thank you."

She was touched he'd remembered the type of wine she liked. Had anyone ever done anything that thoughtful for her before?

She couldn't think of a single instance.

He poured wine into plastic cups and handed her one. Holding his out for her to cheers, he said, "To new beginnings."

"To new beginnings," she echoed automatically.

She'd been trying to distance herself from her past and start fresh—be her own person, not defined by who her family was or what her reputation had been in college.

Taking a sip of her wine, she stared at Luther's profile. Could he be the thing that finally helped her achieve that?

CHAPTER 19

Anna

The glow from her date with Luther hadn't worn off the following day. Anna read another line of the email she'd been working through for the last hour. She kept getting distracted. At the word 'museum,' her mind wandered again back to their date.

While exploring the historic architecture and learning about Stevenstown's history had been thrilling, the real highlight came later.

When the museum closed, the band came in and set up. While they'd shared their food truck dinner, they'd laughed and talked for hours until it got dark. She closed her eyes and leaned back in her chair, recalling dancing under the stars with him.

The band had been local, and though she'd been unfamiliar with their music, she'd enjoyed the mix of lilting notes and fast country beats. He'd proved to be a skilled dancer, dragging her along for a line dance.

She softly chuckled as the joy dancing with him had given her ballooned in her chest. She'd never had so much fun in her life. And it was all because of Luther. He'd curated the perfect date for her and included things she loved.

She was glad she'd opened her gates and let him in. It was a risk, but she was determined to ride the wave as long as it lasted because it felt amazing to have someone take so much care trying to please her. A part of her was still afraid, but it was overshadowed by how happy she felt in his company.

And his kisses. *Mmm.*

She hummed and touched her lips as she replayed the kiss he'd given her last night. It had been another tender one, which started the slow burn low in her belly. Even remembering it, she felt the heat lapping at her. It was comforting to know he could be so gentle, but a part of her missed the storm of their first kiss. And she wanted—

Her eyes popped open at the ringing of her office telephone, and she bolted upright.

Clearing the desire from her throat, she answered the call. "Hello?"

"Anna Hendricks?" a familiar voice asked, and her shoulders drooped.

"Yes."

"Please hold for the mayor." The line buzzed, and Anna sighed. She didn't want to deal with the mayor today.

The bubble of her joy popped as the mayor's voice addressed her. "Anna?"

"Yes, Mayor Landstrom."

What did the unpleasant woman want now?

"I hope I'm not catching you at a bad time, but I wanted to apologize for my nephew." The mayor's voice was heavy on dismay, but Anna didn't understand why.

Did she know the mayor's nephew?

"Your nephew?"

"Yes, Richard—"

She almost dropped the phone. Richard was the mayor's nephew? He'd never told her that!

"—I hope you can forgive him for such a childish prank."

She would've sputtered if she wasn't still in shock. "A childish prank?" She didn't understand how the mayor could think sexual harassment was childish.

"Your tire. It seems extreme to hold someone in jail overnight for that, but either way, I hope we can put this unpleasantness behind us because we all have work to do."

She was impressed the mayor was able to sound sympathetic and condescending at the same time. Still, her words stirred up Anna's outrage.

"Oh, *we* do?" She didn't want any part in the mayor's 'work' and hoped the woman didn't include Richard in that 'we.'

The mayor continued as if she hadn't spoken, "There's a meeting tomorrow night with the Development Review Committee. You're expected to be there."

Fishsticks!

She rolled her eyes and dropped her forehead to her hand. A pit had formed in her stomach at the mention of the meeting.

So, that's the real reason the mayor called. "I'll be

there.”

But under protest.

"Excellent. I'll have the agenda sent over.”

"Great.” She didn't care if her tone was as lackluster as she felt.

"See you tomorrow evening, Anna.”

"Good—” the line went dead before she finished, and she frowned at her phone. What did Mayor Landstrom expect from her at the meeting?

She worried about what might fall out of the dark cloud the mayor held over her.

Groaning, she hung up the phone and dropped her head in her hands. The joy from her date with Luther couldn't outweigh the dread of attending this meeting.

And what was the deal with Richard and the mayor? All the times they'd talked about Mayor Landstrom and her plans for the town, not once did he bother to mention he was related to her! And why would the mayor apologize for him if they were at odds? It didn't make any sense unless it was just another lie he'd told her. *Ugh!*

She slammed her hands down on her desk. She was so sick of subterfuge. Couldn't anyone tell her the truth? She was fuming when a knock sounded at her door.

"What?” she yelled.

The door opened, and Richard poked his head in.

"You!” she snarled and shot to her feet as he entered. He shut the door behind him, but she was angry enough not to feel fear.

"Hello, Anna.” Despite her apparent unhappiness at seeing him, Richard's voice stayed pleasant as he approached her desk.

"Why didn't you tell me you were the mayor's nephew?" she seethed. Her hands clenched into fists, and her breathing was unsteady as she stared him down.

He took a step closer, and her brain screamed he was getting too close. A quiver raced up her spine and woke her from her rage. "Wait, you're not supposed to be here. They'll arrest you again!"

She backed up and hit her chair. At the contact, her legs trembled, but she told herself she wasn't trapped. Moving around it, she put the furniture between her and Richard, adding an extra layer of protection.

He smiled and sat in one of the chairs across from her desk. "That's wholly unnecessary. Anna, please sit." He waved at her chair. "I'm here to explain."

She wasn't about to trust him or fall for any more of his lies. "No."

He shrugged. "All right." He held his hands up in a gesture of apology. "I'm sorry. Slashing your tire was foolish and the least of the things I need to apologize for."

He sighed heavily, and his eyes shone with regret, but she wasn't letting her guard down yet.

"I never meant any of that business about payment in sexual favors."

He shook his head, but she merely narrowed her eyes at him, waiting for the moment he'd reveal the truth of this farce of an apology.

"I only wanted to scare you off, to make you quit."

Her hands gripped the back of her chair as anger stirred in her chest. "Why would you want me to quit?"

"Because this job was supposed to be mine. I've been working with the society for years. I have the knowledge *and* the experience. Unlike you." His voice rose at that, but he took a breath, calming it before he continued, "When the county gave the job to you, a girl barely out of school, I . . . reacted poorly."

"I'd say," she muttered, but she kept her eyes trained on the slippery snake, curious what deception he'd offer her next.

"I slashed your tire in a moment of anger, hoping it would make you late enough to look bad on your first day. It was petty, I'll admit. But I *am* truly sorry for it and the other . . . things I said. I'd hoped they would be enough to make you leave, but"—he smiled, his lips curling sheepishly—"I see, you're stronger than that. And even"—he blew out a breath—"a potentially good candidate for this position."

She would've snorted at his compliment if she wasn't so focused on watching his every move. "Why are you telling me this, Richard?"

"Spending the night in jail was a wake-up call." He ran a hand through his dark hair, then leaned back in his chair. "I like my job, and I'm good at it. I don't want to jeopardize that." His dark eyes locked with hers. "Plus, you're not likely to stay here forever. The big city girl in the small town." He chuckled, but she didn't find that funny. "I can try for the position again when you vacate it."

"So what?" she scoffed. "You want a truce?"

"Yes. This is a small town. We'll run into each other even if we're not working together. And, as you're now aware, I have pull with the mayor." His grin was sly, and she wanted to smack it off his face. "We'd make far better teammates *on* or *off* the field"—he leered at her, making her blood pressure rise—"than being on opposing sides." Finished, he steepled his fingers and stared at her over them.

The nerve of this, this, jerkwad!

Anna wanted to scream at him, but she kept her face calm. "Get out of my office, or I'm calling the police."

He dropped his hands and frowned. "Ann—"

"Out!" Not wanting to hear any more from him, she lost her composure and speared a finger at the door as her chest heaved.

Richard stood, but he didn't move toward the door. His expression was sad as he told her, "You'll regret this."

"I doubt it." She glared at him and started to reach for her phone. He got the message and headed for the door.

"We'll see," he muttered as he left.

Her knees buckled in relief when Richard disappeared. She caught herself by hanging on her chair. Gasping for breath, she could think but one thing.

Luther. She had to tell Luther.

* * * *

Luther

Luther had just stepped under the shower spray when he heard knocking on his door. He rolled his shoulders, sighed, and then turned the water off. The knocks sounded again, more incessant this time, and he cursed. Grabbing a towel, he wrapped it around his waist on his way to the door. Water dripped into his face, and he shook his head to dislodge it. Holding the towel at his hip with one hand, he opened the door with the other.

Anna. He grinned at her, his dimples popping out, and he forgot his annoyance at having his shower interrupted.

Her eyes widened behind her tortoise-shell glasses. "Where are your clothes?"

"You caught me in the shower."

Want to join me?

He couldn't help the thought. As his blood traveled south, an arrow of need pierced him, and his grin faded.

"Oh, um, I can come back." She stepped away, but he didn't want her to leave.

Reaching for her arm, he shook the mental image of them in the shower together out of his head. There'd be time for that later.

"No, it's fine. Come in."

She'd been staring at his chest, and at his offer, she blinked then blushed. "All right."

He loved it when she blushed, the rosy, pink color flooding her pale cheeks. Grinning to himself, he led her to the couch. After he turned off the flat-screen T.V. he'd had on for background noise, he silently thanked his mom for instilling in him a need for tidiness. No half-eaten food or dirty clothes to be embarrassed about here.

When she sat down, he told her. "Give me a sec."

He hurried back to his bedroom to throw on a T-shirt and gym shorts after using the towel to scrub the water off as fast as possible.

She was chewing her lip when he returned to the living

room. The simple action sent his thoughts in a dangerous direction, and he forced himself to look away.

He was trying to take things slow, to give her space to get used to the idea of them together. Seducing her on his over-priced couch was not going to help with that. But the plush leather yielding to their combined body weight was a tantalizing image.

He swallowed and pushed it from his mind. "Do you want a drink? Water? Anything?" he called as he bee-lined for the kitchen.

"No, thank you."

He almost didn't hear her muted response and grabbed two bottles from the refrigerator anyway since he was getting one for himself. After finishing his nightly run, he'd wanted the hydration, but now, he needed it to cool his suddenly dry throat.

He set a bottle in front of Anna on the glass-topped coffee table. "In case you change your mind."

Then he sat on the couch next to her, taking a long swig of his own drink.

He took his first good look at her when she turned to him. A line marred her brow, her eyes were glassy, and she picked at her fingernails.

"Hey." He set his bottle down and moved closer, placing his hands over her fidgeting ones. "What's wrong?"

"Richard came to see me."

"What? When?" His blood pressure spiked, and he had to work to keep his hands gentle on hers when every part of him was roaring to go after Cartwright.

"This afternoon." She took a deep breath before

continuing, "He apologized for the tire and the harassment."

He felt his eyes narrow. Why would Cartwright do that? What was his angle?

Anna frowned, and her eyes were troubled. "He said he was trying to get me to quit. Apparently, he wanted my job and was mad when he didn't get it."

"He may have told you why he did it, but it doesn't change anything." Luther gritted out. "He's still out on bail and ordered to stay away from you." And he'd be sure to remind Cartwright of that when he arrested his ass—again.

"No. Well, maybe?" she sighed. "He asked for a truce, saying he'd wait for me to leave Rolling Brook, then try for the job again."

Luther's chest tightened at the thought of her leaving town, and breathing became difficult. He struggled to get words out through the constriction, choking his airway. "Is that what you plan to do?"

"No!" She shook her head. "I'm not going anywhere. He doesn't get to win."

Hallelujah. At her answer, the rope around Luther's lungs loosened, and he took a deep breath. "Good. What else did he say?"

"That was basically it." She shrugged a shoulder and avoided his gaze.

"He didn't threaten you?" He reached up and tucked her hair behind her ear so she couldn't hide behind it.

At the gesture, her eyes came back to his. They were guarded, and he needed to know why.

"Hurt you?" he asked softly. If Cartwright so much as

laid a finger on her, he'd kick his ass—job be damned.

"He didn't hurt me." Her voice was barely above a whisper. Her eyes were overly bright, and he knew she was fighting tears.

"But he threatened you?" The vein at his temple pulsed as he waited for her answer.

She looked down at their hands and threaded her fingers through his. The simple gesture eased some of the rage filling him. When her eyes met his again, the tears were gone.

"He didn't overtly threaten me. He just made some biting comment about how I'd regret not dropping this."

"That sounds like a threat to me." The pulsing came back, and it wasn't just at his temple as adrenaline surged through his body like a tidal wave. He had a fierce need to protect her . . . at any cost. "I'm going to arrest him, Anna. He violated the terms of the bond."

He stood, intent on going after Cartwright. His vision had tunneled with rage, and he didn't notice her rise with him, their hands still entwined.

"No!" She dropped his palms and fisted his shirt with desperate fingers. "Don't! He was just being a jerk. Please, Luther. Let it go."

He frowned down at her pleading eyes. Why wouldn't she want Cartwright behind bars?

"He'll answer for it in court. I don't want to stir up any more trouble. The mayor . . ." Her voice cracked in panic, and the sound helped him push through the fog of his fury.

He kept his voice even though he still struggled to stay calm and placed his hands on her shoulders. "What about the mayor?"

"They're related. She even called me to apologize for him. If Richard were to go to jail again . . ." Anna shook her head. "She'll hold it against me. Possibly even retaliate."

His jaw clenched as his anger spiked, this time at the mayor. He couldn't believe the woman called to defend Cartwright's actions.

"Dammit!" He stared over Anna's head as he tried to think of a way around the mayor. The woman had pull, and if she got her lawyer to help Cartwright again . . .

He didn't like the odds stacked against them.

"Luther?"

He brought his attention back to her. She was still holding onto his shirt for dear life. Her knuckles were white where she'd gripped them so tight. He took a deep breath, started to count, and gently pressed on her hands as he used his training to settle down.

"Okay. We'll figure out another way."

On a sigh of relief, she closed her eyes briefly, then loosened her hold. He kept her hands in his and used them to pull her into his chest. He locked her arms behind his back before letting go and squeezing her in a hug. She laid her head against him, and he cradled it as he promised he'd do whatever it took to keep her safe.

CHAPTER 20

Anna

Anna breathed in Luther's scent; the notes of orange and something darker—muskier—filled her nostrils and relaxed her tense muscles. She'd been on edge since Richard's visit, but the simple act of telling Luther about it helped ease the strain.

He wanted to arrest Richard, but Anna thought that would do more harm than good. It wasn't her coworker she was worried about. No, it was the mayor she was unsure of.

How would the woman retaliate if she had her nephew arrested again?

Anna shuddered and felt Luther's arms tighten around her.

The Development Review Committee might be the least of her problems. A short while after Richard left her office, she'd received the agenda for the committee meeting. There was a big construction project on it, one she was sure the mayor wanted approved.

She'd spent an hour going back and forth before deciding they couldn't send Richard back to jail because she couldn't afford to alienate the mayor when the woman had the town at her back. Getting preservation projects approved was enough of a battle as it was.

She sighed. She'd worry about the committee tomorrow. Right now, she wanted . . .

Anna bit her lip and felt her face burn. She wanted Luther to help her forget about her problems.

A nervous laugh bubbled up, and she swallowed it. How did she ask him that?

Gawd! This was so embarrassing. And what if he didn't want her? She was hardly a supermodel, and he looked so, so *edible.*

Mmm, Officer Yummy.

She closed her eyes and pictured him dripping wet in only the towel. She'd practically melted into a puddle of liquid lust when he'd answered the door. He was lean but muscled, like someone who spent copious amounts of time in the gym every day while she . . . didn't particularly like working out.

"Fishsticks," she muttered under her breath.

He chuckled, and it reverberated against her cheek. "What was that?"

She pushed out of his hold so she could see his face. The light blue of his eyes sparkled, and his mouth lifted in a half-smile.

Taking a deep breath, she leaped. "I don't want to be alone tonight."

The lightness in his expression faded, and he cupped her cheek. "You can stay here. I'll sleep on the couch."

Great. He doesn't get it.

Her pulse raced at the realization she'd have to just say it. After a breath that did nothing to calm her jumping stomach, she opened her mouth, and . . . no words came out. She tried again but only succeeded in looking like a fish as her mouth opened and closed, opened and closed.

Fudge on toast!

Luther's brow furrowed. "What is it, Anna?" He caressed her cheek, and she grabbed his hand. With a flaming face, she placed it over her breast. At the contact, his eyes darkened and shot to hers.

"No," she managed to squeak out. "I want to sleep with you tonight."

All right. There. She'd said it. Now, if he'd only kiss her before she fainted from embarrassment.

He closed his eyes, but he didn't take his hand away. Shaking his head, he opened them, and they were even darker, the silver overtaking the blue. "You don't have to. I don't want to rush you."

"You're not rushing me." Didn't he want her? What good would waiting do?

Her eyes went wide in realization. He was trying to let her down easy. Her thoughts swirled in a growing tornado as she waited for his response.

"Anna," his voice strangled before he told her, "you're practically a virgin. We should take things slow."

The color drained from her face. Is that what this was about? He wanted someone with more experience.

She blinked against the tears flooding her eyes as the truth speared her heart. "I shouldn't have told you."

She pushed his hand away and would've run, but he caught her. The warmth from his hand on her arm only added to the pain.

He turned her around and lifted her chin. "Don't do that."

"Do what?" she spat at him. Anger was better than hurt, especially if it kept the tears at bay.

"Run away." He kept his other hand on her arm, probably aware she'd be out of there as soon as he let go.

His eyes were so soft, though. If she stared into them for long, she'd drown.

She turned her head, forcing herself to look away. "But you don't . . . want me." Her voice cracked, and the tears spilled over.

"Dammit, Anna, I do." He reached for her chin again and tilted it up. "Look at me."

She met his gaze, and the desire was there in the stormy depths.

"I want you too much. I'm afraid—" He wiped a tear from her cheek. "I don't want to hurt you."

"You won't. Please, just for tonight." She couldn't believe she was begging him to make love to her, but there was a force she'd kept locked away for too long, barreling its way through her. She was tired of being alone. Tired of being afraid. With him, she was neither of those things, and she wanted to know what more they could be . . . together. "Please."

She searched his eyes for acceptance and stood on her

tiptoes to kiss him. They'd turned to smoke, and when her lips met his, he didn't push her away. His hands came to her waist, his thumbs rubbing lazy circles as she applied more pressure. His touch stoked the fire building within her, and she licked the seam of his lips, asking for permission to taste inside.

But he broke the contact, lowering his forehead to hers as he cupped her face. "Anna," he croaked. "You're killing me."

"Then die a happy man." *Whoa.* She was shocked she'd said that. But it was out there now.

A surge of confidence flooded her, and her system went from fifty percent to fully charged. She breathed deeply, praying he didn't push her away again. "Kiss me, Luther. Like you did the first time."

Feeling bold, her hands explored beneath his shirt. As her fingers danced along his sculpted stomach, whatever rein he'd had on his control snapped. She saw it flash in his eyes before his lips crashed down on hers. When they did, she had to grab onto his forearms for balance. Her head spun as his tongue collided with hers. He tasted like his favorite candy, and she savored the fruity flavor.

Mmm, citrusy.

As he deepened the kiss, her knees grew weak. She would have fallen, but he pulled her tight to his chest, holding her in place. They were pressed so closely together that she felt how much he wanted her. It sent a bolt of lightning racing through her, setting all her nerve endings ablaze with the knowledge she was able to do that to him.

When he finally released her mouth, she gasped for

breath, holding onto his arms to keep from falling.

His eyes held her captive, the dark pools swirling with desire. "Is that what you wanted?"

The huskiness of his voice fanned the heat between her legs. She managed a nod. "Do it again."

The storm returned to his eyes, but now it was full of fire. He cursed, and the inferno combusted. When his mouth met hers again, the flames spewed out and licked along her skin.

It's so hot.

She was burning up, but she'd happily turn to char in Luther's arms. Like he had the first time, he hiked up her skirt and lifted her. She wrapped her legs around his waist and moaned against his lips as the contact sent flames crawling toward her center.

He walked her backward to the wall. Being trapped between him and the hard surface delighted instead of frightened her, and she tugged at his shirt, wanting to feel his skin on hers. He freed her lips and helped by pulling the shirt off one-handed.

Hello, Officer Yummy.

She barely had time to take in the muscled view before his lips captured hers again. On a growl, he pushed off the wall. She didn't know where he was taking her but didn't want to lose contact. Her hands raced over every hard, chiseled inch of his chest as he devoured her mouth.

When his hands cupped her bottom, his fingers dug into her flesh while she continued to explore. He stopped walking and pressed her up against the wall in the hallway. With a groan, he broke the kiss and took her breast in his mouth through her clothing. Even with the barrier, it sent flickers of heat hissing through her, and her head fell back.

"Luther." Her breath rushed over her lips at this new sensation.

When he didn't stop, she grabbed his head and lifted his face.

His voice was tight. "Please don't tell me to stop now."

Gulping against the intensity of the firestorm raging in his eyes, she demanded, "Take it off."

At her request, lightning flashed in the depths of his pupils, and he set her on her feet. With a snarl, he ripped open her button-up shirt.

Her eyes widened at the animalistic display, but when he hungrily drank her in as if she was his favorite meal, she thought it was worth the cost of the Hugo Boss blouse.

His eyes flew to hers before he said, "I'm going to taste every inch of you."

Then he shoved what was left of the shirt off her shoulders, undid her bra, and captured her untethered breast in his mouth. The feel of him tasting her drove out any thought but those of pleasure.

When he nipped at her, she gasped. The flames spread from his teeth straight to her core. He soothed the spot with his tongue, then switched to her other breast and gave it the same attention.

A storm rivaling Luther's built within her, and she didn't know how to stop it from erupting. Thunder rocked her as he continued to taste her. It rumbled through every inch of her, and she felt dangerously close to losing control.

He nipped at her again, and lightning struck, sending

charged jolts across her whole body.

Oh. My. Gravy.

She'd never felt anything like it before. The shockwaves continued to crash over her in pulsating succession.

It's too much.

Her eyes shuttered, and her knees gave out. She would've collapsed at his feet, but he lifted her bridal style. His chest was warm on hers, and feeling a little light-headed with gratification, she laid her head against it.

"We're just getting started, Shortcake," he whispered in her ear.

Her eyes flew open, and she stared up at the scruff on Luther's chin as he carried her to his bedroom. She wasn't afraid with him, but her experience with Dan left doubts plaguing her.

Would this next part be as good as what they'd just done, or would it leave her feeling bereft and used as it had with Dan?

When they reached his bedroom, she glanced around. It was laid out identical to hers. The Victorian details were in the wall sconces and plaster ceiling, but his fireplace had a dark aqua pattern compared to her maroon one. He had a book on the mantle, and she smiled, curious about what he was reading.

Her smile morphed into an "O" as he set her down slowly by letting her slide against his body. Thoughts of anything but him went up in a puff of smoke. That definitely still felt good. When she leaned into him, his arousal met her, and she lifted a hand to rub against his shorts.

What does he look like under there?

His hard length jumped at her touch. Her eyes widened, and he growled, lowering his head to bite her bare shoulder. She gasped as electricity buzzed outward from the wound. The heat lightning made her pulse race, and she reached for his shorts while he tugged at her skirt.

"I love your tight skirts, but how do I get you out of this thing?"

"There's a zipper." She moaned as his mouth closed over her breast, and her hand slid from his gym shorts. "At the back."

He found it, and the crackling of her zipper lowering heightened the embers smoldering within her.

As her skirt slid to the floor, he released her and stepped back. She stood before him in only her lace cheekies.

She tried not to feel self-conscious as he stared. The longer he looked at her, the more she wanted to cover herself. She lifted her arms, but he stopped her from hiding.

"Don't." His eyes were molten as he stared her down. "You're beautiful, Anna. I enjoy looking at you." He stepped closer and ran his hands over her. "But I want to touch you even more."

She blushed and reached for his shorts again. "My turn to look."

He helped her push his shorts down, and her lips parted when he was bare before her.

Wow. Her stomach jumped at the thought of putting that inside her. *Will it fit?*

Nervous all over again, her palms started to sweat. She

looked up at him, but he was grinning at her. His dimples flashed as he advanced. When his mouth descended, his tongue dancing with hers, the winds of his passion fanned the flames of hers, burning the nerves into nothing but ash.

He backed her into the bed until they were falling on top of it. Their landing was the opposite of graceful, and it broke their kiss. She bounced into him and started laughing. He propped himself up on his forearms and hovered over her.

Smiling those dimples at her, he said, "I really love your laugh."

She blushed. Her chest felt lighter at the compliment. "And I love these." She traced a finger over each of his dimples.

He lowered those creases to her chest and started pleasuring her again. The heat from the fire smoldering low within her flickered to life. He made his way down her stomach, and each kiss was a hot brand that singed her skin.

When he stopped at her underwear, she lifted her hips so he could slide them off. His eyes never left her body as he slowly pulled them down. When she was bare before him, his eyes lifted to hers, and the desire in them scorched her. She swallowed, dying to know what else he would show her.

He lowered his head between her thighs. When his lips touched the most intimate part of her, she shuddered, and her head fell back. Her hands gripped at the sheets as pleasure sparked through her.

He lifted his head and growled, "I love how responsive you are."

She could only mewl in reply, and his head ducked back down. His tongue joining his lips caused the fire within her to erupt into a roaring blaze. Surely, there was smoke from how hot it was. It fogged up her brain and left her desperate for air.

Too good. That feels too good!

After being left fallow for too long, her body was a dry hillside, and his mouth a brushfire fueling the flames forking up and down her in a frantic inferno. She whimpered as his tongue licked her into a frenzy. The pressure was building again, and it carried a heat too hot to handle. It ignited something deep below her belly that burned hotter and hotter until it snapped. She cried out, her body bowing of its own volition as the flames engulfed her.

When the smoke cleared, she blinked up at Luther. He hovered over her with a satisfied smile.

"I don't think I can move."

He chuckled as he stroked her hair. "You're good for my ego."

She smirked. "I don't think you need any help with that."

A wicked grin spread across his face, and he flipped her onto her stomach.

"Hey!" She laughed, but then his voice was at her ear.

"I'm not done with you yet." His fingers traced down her back, over her hip, and stopped at the juncture of her thighs.

Was he?

Anna wasn't sure how she felt about not being able to see what he was doing, but when his fingers sunk into her, she decided she didn't care. Her eyes closed on a moan as the warmth she was becoming familiar with ignited within her.

"On your knees, Shortcake."

She opened her eyes and sat up to look at him. She'd never . . .

Doggy style?

His eyes were silver smoke, the pupils dark as charcoal. "Trust me?" They seemed to be asking about more than just this moment.

She did, or she was going to—at least in this, at least for tonight. "Yes."

He smiled and helped position her where he wanted her. When she was on her knees in the center of the bed, his body hugged hers as he kissed her neck. She sighed into him, and he gripped her hips.

Equal parts excited and nervous, she held her breath, and he whispered over her shoulder, "Don't tense, baby."

She felt his tip touch her, and she gasped, then blushed in embarrassment. "Sorry," she muttered.

Luther kissed her shoulder. "Nothing to be sorry about."

He eased into her slowly, inch by delicious inch. She tried to relax as her body stretched around him. It burned a little, but the pain only added to the pleasure of feeling him inside her. When he entered her fully, she froze. She was afraid to move.

Oh. My-lanta!

She'd never felt so, so . . . whole. With a contented sigh, she closed her eyes.

Behind her, Luther groaned, "You're so tight." Then he started thrusting.

Her eyes popped open, and her pulse took off. With each piston of his hips, the firestorm she'd seen in his eyes became an electric wildfire that spread frantically, burning its way into her soul. It was unstoppable and all-consuming.

With one of his hands, he rubbed at the bundle of nerves between her legs. She moaned, and his plunges became more rapid. Her breath sobbed out as the fire raged all around her. The sensation of him driving into her while he stroked her was overwhelming. The inferno was coming for her again, and she wasn't sure how long she would last against the intense heat.

His breath hissed out as roughly as hers. "Anna," he ground out, "I'm going to lose it. Come with me, baby."

"I—" Her breathing hitched, and her words became a scream as the orgasm ripped through her. Her arms gave way, but he held onto her hips, plunging into her one, two, more times before he shouted with the thunder of his own release and slumped on top of her.

She sank into the mattress under his weight. It was hard to breathe, but she didn't care. The fire had devastated her. Surely, nothing but residue remained after burning so hot. She hadn't known sex could be this good, or she wouldn't have waited so long to try it after Dan.

Luther grunted and rolled off her. She turned her head to look at him. He smiled at her, his eyes a gleaming blue sky after the gray of the storm.

The smell of the fire they'd created between them was a pungent aroma that hung in the air, and she blushed, thinking of all they'd done.

He chuckled and pulled her into his chest. "What are you thinking about, Anna?"

She tucked her face into his side, trying to hide the blush. "You. Us. I can't . . . I don't . . ."

Gawd! She was stuttering now. She bit her lip and took a deep breath to pull herself together. "That was amazing."

With her head on his chest, she felt his hum of agreement. "We're going to do it again."

She laughed and sat up so she could see him. His eyes were half-closed, and one of his arms was bent, his head resting on his hand. He looked extremely sexy but also very pleased with himself. She found that charming for some reason, and she wanted him again, too.

She shook her head at herself. What had gotten into her? She snorted when her brain supplied the answer.

Oh, right.

Curious how long she'd have to wait, she trailed a finger down his washboard abs.

His eyes opened fully, and he raised an eyebrow at her. "You're playing with fire, Miss Hendricks."

She chuckled. "Oh, I know."

* * * *

Anna

"Can I ask you something?" Anna's head lay on Luther's

chest after the second round of earth-shattering orgasms he'd given her. With her fingers, she traced lazy circles over his abs.

"I need food before we do that again, Shortcake."

She giggled. The thought of making love a third time on the same night should have shocked her, but instead, it filled her with excitement. Her stomach jumped in anticipation, but . . .

"That's not what I was asking."

"Oh."

She sat up so she could see his face. He was grinning, and his eyes were closed. His dimples tempted her to kiss them, but she knew where that would lead. She shook her head at herself. *That* would have to wait. She had a serious question to ask him—about his dad.

She'd been lying in Luther's arms, basking in the afterglow of sex, when she'd realized there were so many things she didn't know about him—things she needed to know. Watching him now and seeing how happy he looked, she hoped broaching the subject didn't make him close down on her. If they were going to be together . . .

No, it was more than that. If he wanted her to trust him, she had to get to know him better.

"Luther?" Her voice came out unsure, and he opened his eyes, his grin fading.

"What is it?" Sitting up, he reached for her hand, lacing his fingers with hers.

She chewed her lip as she stared at the concern shining in his eyes.

Please, don't let this be a mistake.

She took a deep breath and asked, "What happened to your dad?"

His eyes registered surprise before sadness crept in, dulling the silver to gray. She squeezed his hand and waited.

He shut his lids for a second before squeezing her hand back. "He died when I was fifteen. Heart attack."

"Oh, Luther. I'm so sorry." Her heart clenched for him. She may not be close to her parents, but she couldn't imagine what it would be like to lose one of them.

"It's been almost fifteen years, but I still miss him."

His eyes were teary, and she cupped his cheek. "I can't imagine how hard it must've been."

He nodded. "More so for my mom. But she's a strong woman." He smiled softly. "We got through it."

"I'm glad you had each other. I could tell you two were close. I just didn't know why. Not that you can't be close with your mom. It's just . . . um, I mean—" She dropped her hand as her face flushed with frustration at her inability to express this right.

He chuckled, and some of the tension gripping her released. "Relax, Anna." He leaned back and pulled her with him. She settled into his side again as he told her, "He was a police officer, too." She smiled until his voice tightened. "Over twenty years on the force, but his health was what killed him." She felt him sigh. "It made me aware of how important that is, and I've been into fitness ever since."

She winced, glad he couldn't see her expression. From their first meeting, she'd jumped to conclusions about him based on his looks. She wouldn't have been so quick to judge if she knew the reasons behind it. But that was no one's fault but her own.

Kissing the spot where her cheek lay, she said quietly, "Thank you for telling me."

He gave her a squeeze with the arm he had wrapped around her. "I'll tell you anything you want to know about me."

The admission made her smile because she was starting to believe he would. "Good," she murmured against his chest.

Because I want to know everything.

"So, what about your parents? The other night, you said they were in politics, but what do they do exactly?"

Her muscles tightened at the mention of her family. She'd brushed off his questions about them during their date, but now, it seemed only fair to tell him after he'd opened up about his dad.

His hand rubbed up and down her back, and she focused on that to relax herself. He had a right to know. She just hoped it wouldn't change how he felt about her.

Taking a calming breath, she prepared herself to divulge another secret. "My dad's a senator. My mom runs his campaigns."

Luther's hand had stilled at 'senator,' but she was afraid to look at him. She squeezed her eyes closed and braced for his response.

"Oh."

Oh? That's all he has to say?

Her stomach was doing cartwheels, and he was . . .

nonplussed? Dying out of curiosity, she sat up to see his expression.

"Oh?" she asked, raising an eyebrow at him.

He grinned, and his dimples distracted her. She desperately wanted to kiss him there, to lose herself in those creases and forget about her family. Forget all the pressure and expectation they'd leveraged on her for years until she'd felt like she was being crushed under the load.

"Yeah. Now 'Haughty Anna' makes sense."

She blinked those thoughts away, then her eyes narrowed at him. "You think I'm haughty?"

"Only sometimes." He must've noticed the dangerous gleam in her eye because he quickly added. "But I like it."

She shifted and reached for his backside.

"What are you—"

With a quick grab, she pinched him.

"—Ow!"

She hovered her pincers over him, not at all moved by his pretense of pain. "Still think I'm haughty?"

"Yes." His eyes laughed at her, and she pinched him again.

"Hey! This is abuse." He sat up and shook his head at her. "And after all the orgasm—"

"I'll show you abuse." She gripped his flesh a third time and squeezed.

Luther yelped and grabbed her wrists. "Okay, these are in lockup."

She struggled against his hold. When she realized trying to break free was pointless, she put on her best 'I'm in command' voice. "Let go of me."

He laughed. "See. Haughty. Only you can make staring down your nose at someone look hot."

His comment made her insides tingle, but she was still miffed about being called haughty.

An idea occurred to her, and a smile started across her face until it built into a satisfied grin. "You think I'm hot?"

His eyes lingered over her naked body. "Very." His voice was a low rasp that sent a shiver through her, threatening to distract her from her purpose.

Determined to get the upper hand, she batted her eyelashes at him. "Thank you. I want to touch you, Luther." Her eyes focused on his package, and she licked her lips. "Won't you release my hands?" More eyelash batting.

She saw his eyes flicker in consideration before they glazed over, and he let go. "Okay."

Smiling in triumph, she ran her hands up his legs in slow motion. When she reached his thighs, she planned to pinch him again, but he caught her arms and lifted them over her head.

"Hey!" She wiggled, but he had her wrists trapped against each other.

He kept her arms up as he pulled her down with him onto the bed.

"Keep it up, Shortcake, and I'll handcuff you."

Her eyes widened. He wouldn't dare. *Would he?*

But looking into his eyes, she saw that he would—that, in his mind, he already had.

She blushed. The thought of being handcuffed had electricity buzzing through her veins and warmth pooling between her legs.

Before she could ask him about it, his stomach growled loud enough to shake the bed. She laughed softly. "We should eat."

He was staring at her mouth. "Mmm, we should, but I have an idea for dessert."

She would've grinned, except the hunger in his eyes wasn't about food.

Does he really . . . a third time?

She swallowed. "Okay."

His eyes cut to the bag of Skittles on his nightstand.

Wait? He didn't mean . . .?

"Skittles? That's what you want for dessert?" She snickered at his obsession with the fruity candy.

His eyes darkened, and a wicked grin crossed his lips. "Not just Skittles." He winked, and she frowned in confusion.

What did he mean by that?

He gave her a quick kiss on the mouth before he freed her hands and jumped off the bed.

She stared after him, her eyes lingering on his perfectly toned bottom, as he left the bedroom without bothering to put on any clothes.

He hadn't freaked out about her family, and it felt . . . good. Better than good. She smiled as warmth flickered around her heart. She was always afraid of being treated differently when people found out who she was, but Luther didn't care.

"Are you coming, Shortcake?" His voice calling for her broke her out of her thoughts, and she hopped out of bed.

"Coming, Officer Hottie," she called back, then giggled

as the warmth in her chest spread.

Her steps felt lighter than they had in years, as if she were walking off the weight of her past as she made her way toward the future—one filled with many more nights with Luther.

CHAPTER 21

Anna

Anna's anger bubbled like a pot over an open flame in danger of boiling over. She heard her heartbeat roaring in her ears as she stared at the mayor. The letter she'd just given Anna made her blood boil. It was coloring her vision in red, and she worried about what might come out of her mouth.

"*You* did this."

The mayor's expression didn't falter at the derision in her voice.

"Anna, historical or not, that place is an accident waiting to happen. The town building inspector was bound to look at it eventually."

Her chest vibrated with the force of her breaths as she snarled at the mayor, "You had him condemn the property."

Mayor Landstrom frowned at her tone, but she didn't care. "Read carefully, child. Only the dwelling is condemned. The barn you were interested in isn't affected."

That fact didn't mollify her. "Why did you do this?" she demanded, ignoring the mayor's dig at her. "Because I voted against the development project?"

The woman sighed and patted her hair, avoiding her glare. "*I* didn't do anything." She waved at someone over Anna's shoulder. "I'm sorry this news is unsettling, but it can hardly come as a surprise. The farmhouse is practically falling in on itself." The mayor didn't even touch on the fact that Anna stood up to her when she'd accosted her at the start of the Development Review Committee meeting to try and manipulate her for her vote.

Her hand clenched and crinkled the paper that had set her fury on full blast. "It could've been restored. With the proper equipment . . ."

Mayor Landstrom waved a hand dismissively. "I'm not so sure. In any case, the building inspector didn't seem to think so. I believe the letter says you have thirty days to demolish it, does it not?"

Her face flushed in anger at the thought of demolishing a farmhouse that had stood for over two hundred years. She was about to tell the mayor what she'd really like to demolish when a voice stopped her cold.

"Mayor."

Fear at the sound of Richard's voice tempered the fury fueling Anna. Her cheeks paled when he appeared beside the mayor, and she wanted to run away.

Why is he here?

"Ah, Richard. Maybe you can talk some sense into Anna. She seems rather upset over the condemnation of the farmhouse."

"That is a shame, but perhaps it's for the best?" He reached to place a hand on her shoulder, and she instinctively jerked away. He frowned but didn't remark on the gesture. "We try to save as many historic structures as possible, but we can't save them all. There has to be room for progress, too."

He *would* be on the mayor's side.

Her rage returned, and she sneered. "Progress? I don't think destroying a piece of history progresses us anywhere."

The mayor's eyes widened. "Well! It seems you need some time to come to terms with this. I'll leave you to it." On a sharp nod, she left, but Anna didn't feel relieved, not with Richard lingering.

"Why are you here?" She speared him with a look that promised he'd regret it if he tried anything. "You're not even on the committee, and you're supposed to stay away from me until the trial."

"I doubt your case will make it to trial." He shook his head. "I wish you would let this go. We could've been on the same team."

"I see whose team you're on." She crossed her arms over her chest and glared daggers at him.

"Oh, I'm on my *own* team, Anna. No matter what you— or the mayor—thinks." He winked at her.

As if she'd be receptive to anything he said!

She stifled a shudder, but the lid on her rage nearly flapped open. "Right."

"I've got somewhere to be, so . . . I'll see you later, Anna."

She scowled. "No, you won't!"

Before turning away, he tossed one of his slimy smiles at her, and a shudder racked her frame. The man gave her the willies in the worst possible way. Either he was still messing with her, or he was a psychopath.

She had a fleeting thought that perhaps she should look into a restraining order, except Richard hadn't exactly threatened her . . . this time. She shrugged it off. Then she remembered he hadn't told her why he was at the meeting.

Grrr!

She wasn't even sure why *she* was here. An obligation, yes, but a pointless one when no one bothered to listen to her. She'd wasted her breath arguing against the latest development project because the mayor backed it and made sure everyone knew it. The woman had even tried to bribe her into voting for it by offering to support her plan to use the Cooper barn as an event venue if she supported the mayor's plan for apartments—on the same property.

Anna rolled her eyes and headed for her car. She didn't want to spend another second in Town Hall. This evening had started poorly when Mayor Landstrom accosted her before she'd even set foot in the door to tell her if she voted to approve this development project, she'd ensure there was a way they could both get what they wanted for the Cooper property. All they had to do was 'work together.'

Thinking about the exchange, she shook her head in disgust. She wasn't about to be bought and hadn't agreed to the mayor's proposal. Not out of principle, though it had certainly made her want to. She'd refused because she was doing her job.

As a member of the Development Review Committee, she'd looked into the proposed development Mayor Landstrom was backing. It was for a mixed-use structure that would sit on the edge of the historic district. The developer was the same one out of Chicago who'd built the Shoppes at Rolling Brook.

Sure, this new building would provide offices and living spaces, but it would also be a complete contradiction of the town's character, not to mention the local environment.

Anna reached her car and shook her head as she climbed in, still replaying the meeting in her mind. Could she have argued a different angle? Would it have made a difference?

Probably not.

The vote had gone four against one. Despite her reservations, she recognized the town's need for additional commercial and residential real estate. Because of that, she wasn't completely opposed to the plan. She'd only wanted to raise concerns and point out the need for an environmental study since they'd be bulldozing nearly fifty acres of wood. But her suggestion had raised the mayor's hackles, and then she'd gone and served Anna with that stupid letter.

Thinking about the farmhouse being condemned made her hands clench on the steering wheel.

As if I need another problem.

Her stomach burned with barely contained rage, she was in a horrible mood, and she was supposed to meet Luther for dinner.

She let out a frustrated sigh and started the car. At least

he would be a bright spot on this awful evening. Things with her were . . . good.

She rolled her eyes at the understatement. They were way better than good, which scared her—a little. She was developing feelings for him, and the walls she'd built were trembling under their weight. But unlike the Cooper house, those walls were a structure she was looking forward to demolishing.

As she drove toward her apartment building, she vowed to try and save the farmhouse . . . *somehow.*

* * * *

Luther

Luther leaned against his cruiser and crossed his arms as he stared out over the fields of corn. A breeze blew and fanned the leaves already growing on the stalks. They were only half their full height, but they'd be flowering soon. As the cloud cover moved, he squinted against the brightness of the afternoon sun, thankful the department had switched to their white uniform shirts. The rays beat down on him with unrelenting heat. If Sergeant Jameson took any longer, he'd climb back in the car and crank up the air conditioner.

He rubbed his chin as he thought about why he was out there. Last night, when Anna mentioned the same developer of the Shoppes at Rolling Brook was planning a new development in town, alarm bells started ringing in his head. He'd looked into the real estate broker behind the Shoppes deal—Gerald Harding.

The man had his hands in a lot of pies. Not only did he buy and sell properties, but he developed them too. Restaurants, offices, retail, and now he wanted to build apartments?

Yeah, Luther would bet some of those would be rented out to mystery tenants like with the Shoppes.

Even more interesting was the fact that the mayor pushed for this project to go through. It had him wondering just how much Mayor Landstrom knew about the developer.

At the sound of tires crunching over dirt clods, he turned and saw Sergeant Jameson parking his SUV behind his cruiser. When Sarge climbed out, Luther pushed himself off his car and met the man halfway.

The sergeant stopped, cursing, as he patted his pockets, looking for something. "Dammit, I don't have my shades," he muttered as Luther drew near.

Mindful of that, Luther walked to Sarge's other side so he wouldn't be looking directly in the sun. "This will be quick."

Sarge nodded. "Good. What's the update?"

"The town just voted on another project by that same real estate developer." The sergeant gave him 'so what?' eyes, so he continued, "The mayor pushed for it, and the committee approved it."

Sergeant Jameson's gaze became thoughtful. "So you think it'll be another front organization?"

He'd learned to trust his gut; it was telling him yes. "I'd bet my next paycheck on it." His jaw set, and he shook his head. "Seems like the same setup. They'll either rent space to fake tenants or bring in shell companies to launder money."

Sarge just nodded as he processed what he'd told him. "What's your take on the mayor?"

She worried Luther more than he'd like to admit because she was too close to Anna. He didn't want the woman he loved to get caught up in this.

I'm in love with Anna.

The thought didn't make him pause. He'd come to terms with the fact his heart was involved whether he wanted it to be or not. Every time he saw her, the damn thing beat faster, and he couldn't stomach the idea of her getting hurt. If she was in danger—

He pushed down the fear rising up his throat and answered the sergeant. "We already know somebody in the department's involved . . . doesn't it stand to reason they'd be protecting someone higher up—someone who benefits from the developments going in?"

Sergeant Jameson scratched his chin. "It does. But if we're going to implicate the mayor, we've got to have more than conjecture."

He frowned because Sarge was right. "Yeah. I'm working on it."

"If the mayor's involved . . ." The sergeant's face flushed in anger, and he cursed. "It's time to talk to the feds."

Luther nodded. He was thinking the same thing. He also needed to tell Anna to stay away from the woman.

CHAPTER 22

Anna

When Sandy breezed into her office, Anna was pouring over archived newsletter articles on prohibition.

The older woman gave a high-pitched squeal before exclaiming, "I have a surprise for you!" She was carrying a large box, and Anna jumped out of her seat.

"Is that heavy?" She reached for the box and found it wasn't too bad, but she still helped Sandy carry it the rest of the way to her desk.

The older woman clapped her hands when they'd deposited it on top and squealed again. "Open it!"

Anna laughed at Sandy's apparent excitement but hesitated at the thought of what might be in the box. "O-kaaay."

Giving in to the woman's exuberance, she reached for the sharpest thing she had close by—an antique letter opener. It had a lacquered wood handle with a brass blade but was strong enough to slice through packing tape.

Sandy's excitement spewed over as she cut her way into the box. "I can't wait for you to see it! We ordered it months ago, but getting here took such a long time."

She pulled the last of the tape off and opened the box. "Oh, wow."

"I think it'll be a useful tool." Sandy clapped her hands. "We bought it with the last of our grant funds. What do you think?"

The older woman had succeeded in surprising her. Anna stared down at the fancy camera drone. She'd seen them used in the city before but hadn't dreamed of purchasing one for the society. The drone could be helpful in conducting assessments of properties. They'd be able to get a bird's eye view for surveying and mapping, plus drones could go places people necessarily couldn't.

She'd even seen an interactive three-dimensional display of a building created using drone imagery when she was in school. How cool would that be for the Cooper farm?

She lifted her head to meet Sandy's eyes. "This is great. We'll have to figure out how to use it, but you're right; it'll be an excellent tool."

Sandy smiled, and her blue eyes lit up. "Why don't we go to the Cooper property tomorrow and take it for a test drive?"

She returned the smile, but it was half-hearted. Almost a week had passed, and she hadn't gotten any closer to saving the farmhouse. "Sounds like a plan."

* * * *

Anna

When her eyes were ready to cross from staring at image after image of scanned microfiche, Anna decided to call it a day. She'd found a few articles that mentioned prohibition in Rolling Brook, but nothing tied it to the Cooper farm.

With a sigh, she closed her computer. She needed to find something concrete if she was going to use it for a national register nomination. Listing the property on the National Register of Historic Places wasn't a guarantee she'd be able to stop the demolition, but it couldn't hurt. In any case, it would give her a foundation to stand on when she argued to the town against destroying it.

Her eyes landed on the box with the drone in it. She'd set it on the floor next to her desk after Sandy had left. Maybe she should get familiar with it before she and Sandy tried to use it tomorrow. Thinking it would at least be a win if she made the thing fly, she unboxed it.

It was a rotary-wing craft, which meant it'd be able to hover. She was glad since she was positive, she'd have crashed a fixed-wing one. Digging in the box, she pulled out the manual and located the controller.

Yikes. That's complex.

She'd never been one to play video games, and this quad-copter remote looked like a gaming device. It made her frown, but she set it down to start reading the instructions.

A half-hour later, she was feeling confident enough to test it out. Knowing better than to try it inside her office, she stood and gathered her things. It was still early enough she'd have time to practice with it before dark, and the best place she could think of to do that was at the Cooper farm.

*** * * ***

Anna

When she cleared the trees, Anna slowed her car to a crawl as she passed the crumbling farmhouse at the Cooper property. Her heart ached for it. Admittedly, it was in rough shape, but she'd seen buildings brought back from worse conditions. It was possible . . . she just needed a chance to prove it.

Sighing, she parked on the gravel in front of the big red barn. At least this structure was safe from the mayor's clutches. She frowned and shook her head at herself. When had she become such a drama queen?

She'd villainized the mayor in her thoughts, but the woman was just a politician with her own agenda.

Isn't she?

Anna thought back to what Luther *hadn't* mentioned when he'd told her to keep her distance from the mayor. It had to do with a case he was working on, that much she knew, but his caginess bugged her.

On a groan of frustration at being left in the dark, she climbed out of her Camry. As soon as her heels hit the gravel, she realized she should've thought this through more. She should've waited for tomorrow with Sandy when she'd have dressed appropriately.

Shrugging—she *was* already here—she opened her trunk. She was about to reach for the drone when she heard voices.

Her head popped up, and she turned around, searching in the direction she thought they were coming from.

Who else would be on the property, and are they—she tilted her head as she listened—*arguing?*

Her eyebrows furrowed with curiosity, and she made her way toward the sound.

As she got closer, she recognized the mayor's voice. That piqued her interest. She picked up her pace, dying to know what the mayor might be doing here.

The area she headed into was a part of the property she hadn't explored yet. She was on a path beyond the barn that led through the woods. If she hadn't been overtaken by curiosity, she would've worried about snakes in the dense brush on either side of the dirt trail.

Because she was looking ahead and not down, Anna didn't see the rock that nearly sent her tumbling. Her foot twisted as she stepped on it, sending a sharp stab of pain to her ankle, and she winced.

Fudge!

Stopping, she massaged the spot but didn't hesitate to put her weight back on it as she continued looking for the mayor and whoever the woman was arguing with.

She saw a clearing up ahead and hurried toward it— while watching more carefully where she stepped. She didn't want to end up with a sprain. When she reached the edge of the tree line, the voices rose again.

She peeked out to see what was going on before confronting anyone. Less than twenty feet away, the mayor stood with a man Anna didn't recognize. They were next to a small pond, and their voices had carried over the water. But now, she was close enough to hear them clearly.

"One of your dogs is sniffing where it shouldn't be." The unfamiliar man growled.

She couldn't make out his expression from where she stood—she'd left her glasses in the car—but the tone of his voice and the rigidity of his stance told her how angry he was.

"Thanks for informing me," the mayor bit out, "but that sounds like an issue you're better equipped to deal with."

What are they talking about?

"If this cop starts digging too deeply . . ." He let the threat linger before continuing, "I'm not the only one with something to hide."

Not liking where this conversation was heading, she ducked back into the trees for cover but kept her ears open.

"I'm aware of that, Gerald." The mayor sounded calm now. "But going after a police officer . . ."

Her voice trailed off, and Anna imagined her shaking her meticulously-styled head.

"That's not what I agreed to."

"You agreed to do what was necessary to push my development projects in the town. Taking care of this Monroe—"

They're talking about Luther!

She gasped and quickly covered her mouth with her hand. They didn't seem to have heard her as they continued their conversation.

"—is part of that."

"I won't sully my hands with this." Mayor Landstrom's

voice turned shrill.

"Yes, you will. Get rid of this cop. I don't care if you have to put a bullet in his head yourself," the man she'd called Gerald hissed. "Do it. Or our *friend* will hear about your non-compliance."

At the mention of a 'bullet,' Anna's blood started roaring in her ears.

They're talking about killing Luther!

Her breathing accelerated as fear swamped her, and she stumbled backward. She had to get out of there and warn him.

Turning to flee, she got no more than a step before pain exploded in the back of her skull, and the world went dark.

CHAPTER 23

Luther

Luther rechecked his watch and frowned. A steadily growing pit widened in his stomach, filling with unease. He leaned against the counter at Daisy's Diner, the best restaurant in town. It wasn't the best because it was fancy. There were no white tablecloths amongst the bright red booths and stained concrete floor. But it had the best *food* in town—food he'd been looking forward to sharing with Anna.

It wasn't like her to stand him up, at least not without a text—a call—*something*. He checked his phone, but there were no messages. She was now twenty minutes late. Unable to stop himself, he glanced at his watch again.

Make that twenty-two minutes.

"Luther, you've looked at your watch five times in the last few minutes. Is everything all right, boy?"

He turned to the elderly man seated on a red stool next to where he stood. The man's white tufts of hair stuck out from under his faded Chicago Bears cap. It was Mr. Delacourt. Everyone in town knew him. He practically lived at the diner; at least, it seemed that way since he was always there.

While Luther usually wouldn't have minded chatting with the man, his thoughts were swirling down a dark hole. If Anna wasn't here, something had to be wrong.

His expression became pinched as worry set his nerves on edge. He didn't try for a smile, just nodded. "I hope so, Mr. D."

Mr. Delacourt frowned. "Date stand you up?"

His brow wrinkled. "Looks that way, doesn't it?" But he didn't think it was that simple. A quiver in his gut told him otherwise.

Mr. Delacourt clasped his shoulder. "Happens to the best of us, boy." He slid his plate closer to Luther. "Have half my Reuben. It'll help take the sting out."

He managed a small smile. "No thanks, Mr. D." He pushed off the counter. "I'm going to find out where she is."

Mr. Delacourt saluted him as he headed for the door. "Good luck."

Luther said a silent thank you and hoped he wouldn't need it.

When he reached his car, he called Anna, but it went straight to voicemail. Frowning over that, he left a quick message asking her to call him back, then he cranked the engine to head for their apartment building.

If he were lucky, she'd be there. Maybe she'd lost track of time or had gotten held up at work . . . yeah, and maybe pigs could fly.

He ran a jerky hand through his hair. If that had been the case, she would've texted . . . or answered her phone. He prayed he was wrong as the worry in his gut turned into heartburn and seared its way up his chest.

* * * *

Anna

Luther?

Anna thought she saw him in the distance, but he disappeared when she reached for him. She would have kept searching, but a sloshing sound distracted her. It pulled her away from his image and out of the dark. She blinked as consciousness returned, but when her eyes focused, she didn't recognize where she was.

Staring up at the wooden rafters above her head, she struggled to remember what had happened. Evening sunlight peeked through a hole in the roof.

Where am I?

An acrid smell hit her nose, and she gagged.

Is that kerosene?

She hated that smell. Wanting to escape it, she attempted to sit up, then winced as pain radiated through her head. The throbbing cleared the rest of the fog from her brain, and she remembered being at the edge of the woods, listening to the mayor talking about getting rid of Luther.

Oh no!

"She's awake."

Anna gasped and turned to see Mayor Landstrom hovering in a doorway across the room.

Hurt head or not, she wasn't about to face the woman lying on the floor. She clenched her teeth and pushed herself into a sitting position. As she attempted to stand, she was jerked back to her knees. She yelped when they collided with the floor. Someone had tied a rope around one of her ankles and connected it to a post a few feet away.

The mayor stepped inside, followed by a man in a police uniform. At the sight of him, a rush of relief swept through her until her brain caught up, and she processed the fact that he wasn't here to help her.

The officer carried a jug used for storing fuel. He shook it and cursed. "Empty."

If it was empty . . . she realized what the sloshing was she'd heard. He must have covered the outside of the building in it.

"I'm sure it's enough."

Fingers of panic raced up her spine at the mayor's statement. Tears flooded her eyes, and she blinked them away furiously. She wasn't giving up, not when Luther was in danger.

Clearing her throat, she tried to sound calm as she addressed the woman. "Mayor Landstrom, what is going on?"

"You know, Anna. You've become quite the thorn in my side. You're so young, I thought you'd be malleable and smart enough to play the game. But instead, you've challenged me at every turn." The mayor paced as she spoke but stopped and patted her hair before meeting Anna's gaze. Her eyes turned sad as she said, "I'm afraid you brought this on yourself."

Anna's stomach dropped. "Brought what on myself?"

The mayor glanced around the room. "It's a shame, but you dug your own grave." Her eyes were blank when she finally looked at Anna, and their lack of emotion sent a shiver down her back. "Now, you can lie in it."

She refused to think about what Mayor Landstrom was saying. Shaking her head, she pleaded, "This is crazy. Untie me. Whatever you think you need to do—you don't."

"Oh, but I do." The mayor ran a hand along the timber and stone wall. "This building has to go." She turned back to Anna with eyes that were no longer sad. Something desperate stirred in their depths.

She swallowed. Desperate people were dangerous. They could justify anything if it meant achieving their goal.

"And now, you'll go with it."

As the woman's words penetrated, she recognized where she was.

The farmhouse!

So, that was the mayor's plan? To destroy the house and her in it!

"You need to leave."

Anna turned at the sound of the officer's voice. She'd almost forgotten he was there because she'd been so focused on the mayor. Now, as she stared at him, her control snapped.

Panic colored her voice as she begged, "Officer, please! You can't do this! You're supposed to uphold the law." Fear strangled her airways, but she choked out, "Please help me! Let me go!"

Mayor Landstrom disappeared without another word,

and the officer pulled a lighter out of his pocket.

At seeing it, tears burst from her eyes in a horrible body-racking sob. She was going to die, and she hadn't even gotten a chance to tell Luther how she felt about him.

The policeman knelt in front of her, and she stared at him through watery eyes. "Do you want me to knock you out again? Otherwise, this is gonna hurt like hell."

She blinked the tears away, and they slid down her cheeks as she focused on his dark eyes. How could he do this? He was a police officer. "Why?"

He frowned at her. "Why? Because burning alive is probably one of the worst ways to go."

She closed her eyes on a gulp as that image flashed in her mind. When she opened them, he was still squatting in front of her. "No. Why are you doing this?"

He raised an eyebrow. "Why is the mayor? Why does anyone?" He laughed as if the answer were obvious. "Money, sweetheart."

She flinched at the endearment, and he sneered. "Oh, that's right. You're Monroe's sweetheart, aren't you?" He stood and flicked the lighter open. "Well, don't worry. He'll be joining you soon enough."

Fear for Luther made her face turn ashen. Her breathing quickened, and black spots colored her vision. She clutched her chest and shook her head to clear it.

The officer grabbed a piece of wood from the pile on the floor where the roof had collapsed. At the door, he lit it with his lighter. The spark slowly burned the board, but the man held the lighter in place until the flame spread and caught fire.

As she watched, tears tracked down her cheeks in silent salty streams. "Please."

He ignored her plea and stepped through the door. When he closed it, it banged shut loud enough to make her jump.

She was sitting in a building soaked with kerosene, and the cop was about to light it on fire. Her fear turned into terror. It seized her lungs, and her breathing intensified.

I don't want to die!

Her heart raced, and her pulse pounded so loudly in her ears that she didn't hear the flames at first. But as smoke drafted in through the wall planks, she heard a fire crackling, eating hungrily through the fuel-drenched wood.

I have to get out of here!

She had to think. Panicking wasn't going to help her. She clenched her jaw and forced herself to take a deep breath until she'd swallowed down enough fear to focus on looking for a way out. She saw flames licking up the walls on all sides of her. But the roof. The fire hadn't spread there yet. If she made it up to the hole, she could get out.

She glanced around the floor for anything she might climb on and stopped searching on a cry. She'd forgotten her leg. With shaking fingers, she pulled at the rope around her ankle. The heat from the fire added to the heat of her struggles, and perspiration drenched her. Her eyes started to water from the smoke, but she tugged as hard as she could . . . to no avail.

Though she pulled hard enough on the rope for it to cut into her fingers, it didn't loosen. Coughs racked her chest, and she dropped the restraint, gasping for breath through the dense gray haze filling the room.

I can't breathe!

The dark was coming for her again, creeping in slowly at the edges of her vision. She couldn't fight it off, and as her eyes slid shut, she prayed Luther would be safe.

CHAPTER 24

Luther

Fear had hardened Luther's stomach into a rock by the time he turned onto the road leading to the Cooper farm. He'd gone to Anna's apartment and the historical society, but she hadn't been at either location. When he'd tried calling her again, and she still didn't answer, he knew something wasn't right. His gut told him she was in trouble, but he had one more place to look for her before he accepted that.

She'd told him about her project with the farm, and it was the last spot he could think of that she might be. He was calling in a favor and tracking the GPS in her car or phonc if shc waan't there. Whatever he needed to do.

As he drove closer to the property, the scent of smoke filled the cruiser. He looked for the source, but the tree branches full of green leaves were dense enough to hide it from view. The smell made his adrenaline spike. It didn't make sense for someone to be burning anything on the farm. Not this time of night and not when the place was abandoned.

When he cleared the trees, the farmhouse filled his view. It glowed an angry orange as forked flames ate at the centuries-old wood. The stone in the construction had slowed them down, but the blaze smoldered on.

Time moved in slow motion as two things occurred to him.

Anna's car was here.

She was in that building.

He blinked and slammed his foot on the accelerator. Time sped forward, and so did his heartbeat as he raced toward the house.

When he was close, he stopped, jumping out of the cruiser with only one thought.

Anna. He had to save Anna.

He refused to believe she was anything but alive. Fear for her safety threatened to make his hands shake.

Pushing it away, he focused on what he needed to do to get her out of there. He grabbed a blanket and his emergency kit from the trunk of his car, but it wouldn't do much good against the flames licking at the front door. At least not *dry.*

He needed water. He glanced around in a frantic state until his eyes fell on a barrel next to one of the outbuildings. If it was hollow, it might be filled with rainwater. He ran toward it.

When he reached it, his breath burst out in relief. With jerky movements, he dunked the blanket and soaked up as much rainwater as possible.

With the blanket saturated, he turned back to the house.

Taking a deep breath, he draped the cover over his head and shoulders, then said a quick prayer before doing the craziest thing he'd ever done in his life.

Luther ran full tilt toward the front door with a roar matching the fire's. He crashed through and immediately hit the ground. The door fell from its hinges behind him, and smoke billowed out. It choked him, and his eyes watered, making it hard to see. Holding the blanket over his mouth and nose, he crawled forward, searching for Anna.

After a few feet, his hand connected with her arm, and he shook her, yelling her name. She didn't respond. He would have to carry her out. He coughed as he moved the blanket to cover her head. Grabbing underneath her legs and back, he attempted to lift her.

Something stopped him, and he set her back down, reaching to see what she was stuck on with his hands. When he found the rope at her ankle, rage filled him. He'd suspected the fire was deliberate, but this confirmed it.

Whoever did this is going to pay.

As quick as he could, he found the rescue knife in his emergency kit and sawed at the rope. The fire snapped around them, but he didn't let it stop him. He was going to save Anna or die trying. The restraint gave way, and he scooped her up.

I've got you, baby.

Closing his eyes, he ran out of the house. He stopped running when the steam from the blanket burned his back.

He tossed it to the ground with a growl, then laid Anna down.

Clear of the smoke, he saw her face was covered in soot, her hair matted with sweat. He felt for her pulse. It was there, but it was weak. *Too weak.*

She had to have smoke poisoning. He laid his head on her chest to check her breathing, and he howled in agony when he didn't feel it move. "Noooooo!"

But he refused to give up on her. He was trained in CPR. He could save her.

He started compressions, and his voice broke as he told her, "Stay with me, Anna."

Adrenaline surged through his veins as he pressed hard and fast on her breastbone. Terrifying thoughts—thoughts of a future without her—wanted to cripple him, but he pushed them away and focused on counting.

At thirty, he tilted her chin up and blew into her mouth. The air filled her lungs, making her chest rise, but she didn't start breathing on her own. After another rescue breath, he went back to compressions. The numbers rolled by quickly in his head until he was breathing for her again.

"Come on, baby. Breathe." Silent tears tracked down the soot on his face as he started another round of chest compressions.

When he'd completed the fifth cycle of breaths, he froze at the unmistakable feel of a gun muzzle pressed to the back of his head.

"You're not doing her a favor, Monroe. Suffocation seems better than burning."

He recognized the voice. "What are you doing, Haines?"

Except he knew. Red filled his vision as he understood Officer Haines had done this to Anna.

But why? How does she factor into the money laundering scheme?

Haines didn't answer his question. "Why don't you stand up, nice and slow, and keep your hands where I can see them."

No, I can't. Anna!

He stared down at her, and his heart broke, shattering into a million tiny pieces. The shards, as sharp as glass, sliced into his chest. He didn't want to stop CPR, but he couldn't save her if he had a bullet in his head.

Breathe, baby, please.

He silently begged her as he did what Haines asked.

The gun stayed trained on Luther's head as he got to his feet. "If you shoot me, Haines, they'll know it was murder."

"Not if all they find is ash. That's why we're going to the farmhouse."

He glanced at the building out of the corner of his eye. It was now a blazing inferno. If he stepped foot in there, he wasn't coming out.

"What will the captain say when your gun shows up as the murder weapon?" He needed to keep Haines talking and stall him until he could get the upper hand.

"First, it's not gonna. And I think the captain *and* the mayor will thank me. You're a problem, Monroe. I'm fixing it. Hell, I may even get a promotion out of this." He laughed and jabbed the gun in Luther's back. "Now, walk."

He took a step and stopped. "So the captain's working

for her?"

"We all work for someone, don't we?" Haines pushed the barrel of his gun into Luther's kidney, and he winced. "Move it."

He took another step. "Whose money are they washing?"

"You know what? You ask too many questions. But I'll tell you since you're about to burn to death." He paused for a breath. "Gerald Harding."

The real estate guy.

He wasn't surprised by that. He did wonder where the illicit money came from, but it was a question for the feds to answer.

"If you don't start walking, you're going to be making the trek with a bullet hole right here." Haines moved the gun to his right shoulder and shoved it.

Luther tensed. His whole body was ready for fight mode, but then he heard the only thing that could meld his heart back together.

Anna gasped out a breath, and he took advantage of the distraction to whirl on Haines.

Moving out of the line of fire, he reached for the weapon and twisted, but Haines didn't let go. *Dammit!*

The man fired off a shot as Luther manipulated the bastard's wrist to take him to the ground. It went wide somewhere past the farmhouse.

He bent Haines's wrist until he gained control of the weapon, then pointed it at him. "Cuff yourself."

The man was seething, and his eyes snapped at Luther. "No."

"Do it, or you'll be the one sporting a bullet hole." He

aimed at the man's leg. He wanted to shoot the bastard in the chest for what he'd done to Anna, but he was more valuable alive. The captain and the mayor were still untouched.

He became aware of Anna coughing and hacking as he kept his eyes trained on Haines. The dirty bastard finally complied, and Luther reached for his phone.

He dialed nine-one-one, but calling for help was unnecessary. He could hear sirens in the distance.

The smoke must be visible from town by now.

"This isn't over, Monroe. The captain will have my back." Haines snarled at him, and spittle coated his lips.

"Then you don't have anything to worry about, do you?" He aimed the gun at Haines's chest. "So, stay put."

When the operator answered his call, he gave her a brief rundown of the situation. She confirmed units were already responding to the smoke.

Without taking his eyes or the weapon off Haines, Luther hung up and walked over to Anna. She was still coughing. Her throat had to be swollen, but she was breathing, and that's all that mattered. "Anna, baby. Help is on the way."

"Luther."

It was a hoarse whisper, but he answered. "Right here, baby."

"How?" She pulled in a wheezing breath, and he hushed her.

"Shh. Save your voice, sweetheart."

His finger was twitchy over the trigger. He could focus on her if he didn't have to worry about Haines. Desperate enough to hold her in his arms, to *feel* she was really all right, he considered shooting the other man. Just in the foot so he wouldn't run away.

Anna coughed again, and out of the corner of his eye, he saw her whole body shake with the force of it.

The ambulance needs to hurry the hell up!

As soon as he thought it, the sirens grew louder. He chanced a quick glance behind him to see a fire engine emerge from the trees. A police cruiser and ambulance weren't far behind.

He'd never felt more grateful to see those flashing lights.

"Help is here, baby." *Help is here.*

CHAPTER 25

Anna

The first thing Anna noticed when she woke up was someone held her hand. It gave her a sense of comfort and even familiarity as calluses brushed her palm. Didn't she know that hand? Something beeped in repetition, and she sensed it was bright wherever she was. Wanting to find out *where* that was, she struggled to open her eyes, but her lids were unusually heavy.

That's strange.

She managed to make them flutter, and a voice she recognized said her name as she did. "Anna!"

Luther.

She smiled. Well, she thought she did, but she wasn't sure her expression relayed it. She felt fuzzy—uncoordinated.

"Wake up, baby." He kissed her hand, and she wanted to do as he asked with every fiber of her being.

It took some effort, but she pushed through the fog

surrounding her and forced one eye open, then the other.

There he was. *Officer Hottie.*

"It's good to see those gold eyes again." He grinned at her, but *his* eyes held unshed tears.

Why is he upset? Has something happened?

She reached for his cheek and found her arm was hooked to an IV. Her forehead creased in confusion.

"Luther?" Her voice sounded strange to her ears, and her eyes widened.

"Shh, you're all right. But your throat's probably sore."

"Why?" she croaked out.

"Do you remember what happened to you?"

She was about to shake her head when the fire flashed in her mind. As her memories flooded in—being trapped, waking up outside, arriving at the hospital—the beeping from the heart rate monitor increased.

"You're safe, baby," he soothed, and she closed her eyes to try and calm her thoughts.

The last thing she remembered was the doctors telling her she needed to be put to sleep to heal her scorched airways.

How long ago had that been?

Desperation seized her, and her eyes flew open as she squeezed Luther's hand. "How long?" She took a shaky breath. "Was I out?"

His eyes pinched, and anguish flickered in them. "Five days."

She gasped, and the monitor spiked. *Five days?*

How had she lost five whole days?

"Your body needed time to heal." He took a deep breath,

and his voice was rough as he told her. "You were intubated and under anesthesia."

She swallowed as she digested that, and her throat protested. "Water," she squeaked.

He let go of her hand and reached for the paper cup on a tray next to her hospital bed. When he put the straw to her lips, she grabbed for the cup, sucking greedily.

"Whoa, slow it down, sweetheart."

She stopped drinking and pursed her lips at him. *Why?* She was so thirsty.

He must have noticed the 'are you kidding me' look she was giving him because he explained, "The nurse said little sips. Too much at once, and you risk making yourself sick." He frowned. "Throwing up could do more damage to your throat."

Oh. She understood, but it didn't mean she liked complying. She took another few slow sips until she'd had enough to soothe her dry throat. "Thank you."

He placed the water back on the table. When his eyes met hers again, they were the bright silver color she loved, but they were guarded. Looking into them made her stomach hurt. Whatever had happened—it wasn't over yet.

She reached for his hand, and he clasped it. "What is it?"

"We still need your statement." With his free hand, he brushed her hair off her face.

The simple gesture warmed her heart, and she nodded. She'd get through anything with him at her side. "I don't know where to start."

He gave her hand a gentle squeeze, then smiled in

encouragement. "What were you doing at the farm? Start there."

She took a steadying breath and launched into the story. When she got to the part about being struck in the back of the head and knocked out, his hand tightened on hers. Because she watched him closely, she noticed his jaw set. Trying to soothe him, she placed her other hand on his as she told him about waking up in the farmhouse and her conversation with the mayor.

"We brought her in but without enough evidence to charge her . . ." His jaw clenched, and he shook his head. "She's out. But with what you just told me, we can fix that."

Some of the tension gripping her insides loosened. "What about the officer and the other man the mayor was talking to?"

"Officer Haines is in jail, but he deserves worse for what he did to you." He closed his eyes as if he couldn't bear to think about it, and she realized she didn't know the whole story.

She'd passed out—had been sure she was going to die in that burning house, but, somehow, she'd woken up outside.

"Luther." She pressed her hand to his cheek, and he opened his eyes. They were swimming with emotion—anger, pain, love.

Love. She smiled as she let the feeling crumble what was left of her walls. "How did you know where I was?"

"I checked your apartment and the society. It was the only other place I could think of that you might be. But if I'd gone there first . . ." His voice cracked, and his eyes looked tortured. "You weren't breathing when I found you. I thought . . ." He drew in a ragged breath. "I thought I lost you, baby," he whispered.

He saved me.

As she continued to stare into his eyes, her heart clenched at the pain she saw in them. It had cost him to see her like that. "Thank you for saving me."

"Anna, I—" He shook his head, and she wished she could wipe the bad memories away.

"Come here." She tugged on his hands, but he hesitated.

"You're sore. I don't want to hurt you."

She pushed herself up so she was sitting, and then she opened her arms. "I don't care. Get over here."

He moved to sit on the edge of her bed, and she wrapped her arms around him, laying her head on his chest. She breathed in his familiar citrus and grass scent until she noticed his arms weren't returning the embrace.

She tilted her head up to look at him. "I'm not *that* fragile." After nearly dying, she was through with being cautious when it came to him. "Hold me like you mean it."

His eyes burned hot for a second before she saw him let go. He pulled her close and buried his nose in her hair.

She felt him shaking, and it broke her heart. "I tried to get out—to warn you. I couldn't stand the thought of them going after you." She took a deep breath. "I love you, Luther." Tears clogged her throat, but she swallowed past them. "I thought I wasn't going to get to tell you." Her voice broke into a sob, and he stroked her hair.

"I love you too, baby. So damn much." He paused and

squeezed her tighter. "When I thought I wasn't going to get to tell you, . . . it killed me."

She tightened her arms around him as his words healed her damaged heart. Wiping her eyes on his shirt, she asked, "What happens now?"

He kissed her head before he pulled back and brushed the rest of the tears from her face. "We'll take care of the mayor. She won't get another chance to hurt you."

Anna nodded and waited for him to tell her the rest.

"The conversation you overheard . . . it sounds like she was arguing with the real estate developer of the new project the town just voted on."

Her eyes widened. *What did that mean?*

"My suspicion is she's been helping him launder money through the developments. I'm guessing for kickbacks." He shrugged. "But they use the properties as fronts to wash the illicit cash. That kind of thing draws attention, and Officer Haines and our captain were keeping the heat off."

"Oh!" She covered her mouth with her hand. It was worse than she'd thought. Not only the mayor but also the police captain was involved.

"Yeah," he shook his head. "The captain's been suspended while Internal Affairs conducts its investigation, and the FBI is going after Gerald Harding—the developer." He cupped her cheek. "Clearing this up will take a while. Several local businesses in the Shoppes development were shell companies involved in the laundering, but that's not for you to worry about." He paused, and his eyes held hers. "You'll likely be asked to testify against the mayor, but I'll be with you every step of the way."

She smiled at the determination shining in his eyes. With Luther by her side, she could face it. His love had washed away the blight of her past, and she was ready to build a whole new future with him. "Good. Because I've got plans for you, Officer Hottie."

He grinned, his dimples winking at her, and the weight he'd been carrying since she'd woken up cleared from his eyes. "Me too, Shortcake."

She laughed, but it turned into a moan as his lips came down on hers. As Luther kissed her, a sense of euphoria filled her, and her heart and head reeled. In his arms, she was complete. Together, they could take on anything. So, bring it on, world.

I'm ready.

EPILOGUE

Ten Months Later

Anna

Anna's stomach contracted into a tight ball of nerves that bounced in excitement. She rubbed a hand against it to ease the discomfort as she stared across the property. It was hard to believe this day was finally here.

After everything that happened with the mayor, the town had been sympathetic to her plans for the Cooper farm, and today was the debut event for Yeoman's Hall. She smiled as the Edison bulb lights strung across the property winked on, illuminating the darkening sky. Once the sun set, it would look magical.

From where she stood in front of the refurbished barn, she could see the way to the pond where she'd overheard the mayor so many months ago. She'd had the path widened and the brush cut back. They'd found a stream that fed into the pond and built an arched wooden bridge across it. She thought it added to the charm they'd restored to the property.

As did the white gazebo she'd had built beyond the outbuildings. Picnic tables and benches surrounded it, inviting people to sit for a spell and soak up the fresh air. She envisioned it filled with musicians for an evening concert. Not a bad idea going forward and something she'd add to the website offerings.

People were starting to arrive, and the hum of voices echoed around her as she continued her survey. The air of neglect, which had once lingered here, was gone. She'd had the remaining buildings stabilized and the debris left behind by years of occupants cleaned out.

Her heart squeezed when her eyes fell on the spot where the farmhouse used to stand. She hadn't been able to save it, but she'd commemorated it. The rubble trench foundation showed the outline of where it had stood, and she'd added a marker with the house's history. She'd even found an old photograph in the town archives and had it printed on the plaque.

"There you are, Anna!"

She jumped at the greeting, then chastised herself for getting lost in her thoughts.

"Hi, Sandy. Or should I say, Mayor Redland?" She grinned at the older woman whom she'd come to call a friend.

After Mayor Landstrom was convicted, the town elected Sandy. With the bubbly brunette on the job, getting preservation plans approved had become less of a struggle.

She smiled and shook her head. "You know I prefer Sandy. It's almost go time, dear, and I wanted to make sure you were ready."

She turned with her and took in the *pièce de resistance*—the barn. It was no longer a faded, splotchy red. Now, it glistened a bright white in the waning light of this spring day. The trim and doors were a contrasting black, as were the double barn lights she'd had installed above them. It was gorgeous, and that was only the outside. "More than ready, Mayor."

Sandy chuckled and gave her hand a quick squeeze before heading toward the stage they'd set up inside.

Anna smiled after her. She was glad to have the ladies from the historical society here to support the opening. Not having Sandy on the team any longer had been a blow, but she'd placed the open position with the county and looked forward to filling it. She planned to give them some of Richard's previous duties. With his aunt convicted, he'd left town to escape the stain. Her case against him hadn't gone to trial, so she was happy to be rid of him.

For once, Murphy had taken his law elsewhere, and she felt like her life was finally flowing smoothly. Smiling bigger at the thought, she followed Sandy into the building, running her hands along the repainted stalls she'd turned into exhibits about the property's history.

She'd been able to corroborate the prohibition connection, and with the help of the funds her parents had donated after her ordeal, she'd purchased state-of-the-art equipment that offered a virtual reality experience to visitors. People entered the exhibit and stepped into history as a bootlegger. She'd tested it so many times she'd lost count, but she never got tired of hearing the hiss of the still.

As she walked by, she noticed people inside, staring intently at the images flashing on the walls. It warmed her heart to be able to share this with the town.

But nerves persisted.

She hoped Yeoman's Hall was well received. It was the first of many preservation projects she wanted for Rolling Brook, and whether they approved or not was bound to influence her future success.

When she entered the large open area of the barn, an arm snaked around her waist and pulled her up against a rock-hard body.

She laughed and leaned into Luther as he kissed the nape of her neck. "Break a leg, Shortcake."

She turned in his arms and gave him a quick kiss. "Thanks. But, fudge, I'm nervous."

He grinned, and she traced a dimple with her finger. She never got tired of looking at those.

"This place is amazing. Everyone I've talked to has complimented it *and* you. You've got nothing to worry about, baby."

She gave him another kiss, this one not so quick. "Mmm, thank you."

Someone cleared their throat behind her, and she turned, blushing to see Sandy waiting on her.

Oops. Got to go.

"Showtime." Sandy winked, and Luther gave her one

more squeeze before she followed the mayor to the stage they'd set up at the back of the barn. People filed into seats as she reviewed what she planned to say.

When everyone had settled, she took a deep breath and approached the microphone.

Okay, this was it. They'd either love it or hate it.

* * * *

Luther

This was it. Luther grinned at Anna from the front row of seats as his girl welcomed everyone to the event. What she'd done with the Cooper farm amazed him. He was so proud of her, especially after everything they'd gone through since the horrible night he'd almost lost her.

He rubbed at his heart as the pain of remembering it squeezed his chest in a vice. At least that was behind them now. Mayor Landstrom had been convicted and was in prison. She'd helped the feds take down Harding and his associates for a lesser sentence, but she still wouldn't be getting out anytime soon.

Anna's comment about bootlegging sent a chuckle through the crowd, and he smiled. The money laundering had scarred the town, but it was slowly starting to heal.

Though he hated Mayor Landstrom for what she did to Anna, he appreciated she'd helped take down Harding. The former mayor had testified that the real estate mogul was renting space to fictional tenants and using businesses like the pizzeria as shell companies to wash cash for a known drug trafficker. It was the reason Harding had stakes in so many different ventures. Each real estate purchase was bought for a drug kingpin, but Harding titled the purchases in his own name and submitted fake proof of funds letters during the settlement process. That way, the dirty money was cleaned, and he got to keep the commissions from the sales.

He clapped when Anna finished her welcome speech. She was glowing, and he wanted to make this night even more memorable for her. His stomach jumped with nerves as he brushed the ring box in his pocket. They'd been together nearly a year, and he knew she loved him, but would she be content to live out their lives in Rolling Brook?

She was still a city girl at heart, and he wasn't sure she would settle for the small-town life with him.

He swallowed as the appetizer he'd sampled tried to come back up. He wanted her to. That was for sure.

His mom was here, his friends, his job. But if Anna didn't want to stay, he'd leave. As long as it meant he'd be with her.

Because as much as he loved his hometown, he loved her more.

A large hand clapped him on the shoulder, and he whirled, pulled from his thoughts.

He smiled when he saw who wanted his attention. "Sarge, thanks for coming out."

Sergeant Jameson's smile was sheepish, and he leaned in to whisper conspiratorially. "You're welcome, but I'm here for purely selfish reasons." He chuckled and reached for his wife, who faced away, talking to someone else.

He turned Daisy around, and Luther got his first glimpse of their new baby. She was sleeping soundly in her mother's arms. Her hair was a shock of coal-black like her mother's, and her skin a rosy alabaster. She'd gotten her father's ginger complexion.

Grinning at the little cutie, he traced a finger over her soft, cherubic cheek. "Great job, Mama. She's beautiful."

Daisy smiled and murmured a thank you, careful not to wake the baby.

Sarge protested, though. "Hey, I had something to do with it."

The comment made Luther laugh aloud, but he stopped abruptly at Daisy's evil eye. *Right. Quiet.* He cleared his throat. "What's her name?"

"Abigail."

He stared at the tiny bundle, who already sported a pink bow. "It suits her."

Daisy smiled, and her dark blue eyes sparkled. Luther wondered whose eyes the baby had gotten. Too bad they weren't open to see.

"Monroe," Sergeant Jameson drew his attention away. "Think I can get a minute with your lady? I have an event I want to run by her."

He scanned the crowd for Anna. There she was. Talking to his mother. "That depends. Am I invited?"

"Sure as hell are. Daisy wants to throw me a promotion party."

He would've whooped with excitement, but he caught himself, mindful of the baby. "That's great, Sarge! Or should I say 'Lieutenant' now?"

"Well, it's not official yet. Feels like a long time coming, though. I'm relieved this business with the captain is over."

The mention of their previous captain brought a frown to both men's faces. Luther was glad the corrupt Captain Grouse was gone. He'd turned out to be just as dirty as Haines, accepting bribes from the mayor to keep their dealings under wraps.

"I wonder who they'll bring on as the new captain."

Sergeant Jameson shrugged. "Anyone's got to be better than Grouse."

He nodded and hoped it would be someone they knew and trusted. "True. All right, let's go talk to Anna."

Two hours later, the crowd from town had dispersed, and he was helping her clean up.

"What a night!" She collapsed into a chair and pulled her high heels off.

He grinned at her. The night wasn't over yet. "I'd say the first event at Yeoman's Hall was a success."

She rubbed her feet and groaned. "Gawd, my feet are tired." Then she grinned and looked up at him. "But definitely a success. Nearly twenty people asked me how to book an event here." She jumped up with a squeal. "I just knew this was going to work." Whirling in a circle with her arms outstretched, she said, "The town needed this."

He stopped her twirl and pulled her close. "And I need you."

She chuckled. "Lucky for you, you've got me."

Hopefully for good.

He lowered to one knee, and her brow furrowed. "What are you doing?"

Her eyes went wide when he pulled the ring box out of his pocket. "Are you . . ."

He ignored the roiling of his stomach and prepared himself to ask the most important question of his life. "Yes, Shortcake, I am."

Her hand flew to her mouth. "Oh!"

He took a deep breath and launched into his pitch. "Anna Hendricks, I know we come from different worlds, but mine doesn't exist without you in it." That made her eyes soften. "I think I've loved you since your Skittles-scented perfume first drove me wild." Okay, he could do better than that. He cleared his throat. "Will you do me the extreme honor of agreeing to be my wife?"

She laughed, and he hoped it was a good sign. She cupped his face in her hands and smiled. "If you do me the 'extreme honor' of agreeing to be my husband."

Luther grinned. "That's a yes, right?"

She kissed him, then pulled back with a laugh. "Yes."

His heart felt like it might burst. He grabbed her close and stood with her in his arms. "I love you so much, Anna Hendricks."

She smiled as her feet dangled in the air. "I love you so much, Luther Monroe." Quirking a brow at him, she asked, "Now. Don't I get a ring?"

He grinned. All was right with his world, and he was looking forward to *their* future. He set her on her feet so he could put the ring on her finger.

"Yes, sweetheart. You absolutely do."

A NOTE TO READERS

If you enjoyed this book, please consider leaving a review. They help spread the word about my books through the recommendation process and help new readers decide if they'll be a good fit for them. Reviews also contribute to my rankings on sites like Amazon, making my stories more visible to new readers. Even a one-line review makes a difference!

If you can't get enough of Rolling Brook, pick up the last book in the series, *Marked as Queen of Hearts*. Remember Detective Alonso? Well, he's no longer a detective but the new police captain of Rolling Brook. He might've left Chicago behind, but it doesn't seem to be through with him. His past comes calling in more ways than one when his old flame shows up in town. Can he keep her safe *and* win her heart? Read it and find out! And, of course, there are more cameos from our beloved Redlands!

If you'd like a free novella set in the Rolling Brook world, subscribe to my newsletter. By signing up, you receive an

EXCLUSIVE book featuring a woman on the run and forced proximity with a troubled military hero.

Want more updates, teasers, and giveaways? Follow me on social media.

All my links can be found here: https://linktr.ee/blyedonovan.

Thank you for reading!

xoxo,

Blye Donovan

ACKNOWLEDGMENTS

I want to thank my fellow indie-romance authors—the ladies from Shades of Romance and the Women Who Write Romance. Our community is so supportive, and I am humbled to be a part of it.

For help with technical questions, I'd be remiss if I didn't call out two amazing Facebook groups: Cops and Writers & Authors Fire/Rescue. Your advice was invaluable, and any liberties taken for the sake of fiction are entirely my own!

My critique group. Dream Team ladies, your suggestions are always spot on! This book would not be what it is without your input. Thank you, thank you, thank you!

Lastly, a great big, humongous thank you to all the readers who have fallen in love with the Rolling Brook Protectors. Your support brings a smile to my face, inspiration to my soul, and motivation to keep me sitting in front of the keyboard every day.

BOOKS BY
BLYE DONOVAN

Rolling Brook Protectors

Hunted at Whiteford Farm
Gifts from a Stalker
Small Town Frame-up
Condemned by Secrets
Marked as Queen of Hearts

Stand-alone Novels

Undercover Santa
Blaze of Glory

Texas Heat Shared Series

Wait for You

TOP Security Series

Going Rogue

ABOUT THE AUTHOR

Blye Donovan is a military brat and a veteran who resides in the Lowcountry of South Carolina with her husband and fur-child, Maximus. Besides books, she's addicted to coffee, peanut butter, and shoes. When she's not feeding these addictions, she writes books that are romantic suspense stories featuring strong heroines and alpha protector heroes overcoming dangerous villains. Her books are often set in small towns because she loves the atmosphere associated with them, especially when they  have historic architecture. She was supposed to become a historic preservationist, but . . . writing has always been her passion. You can check out her current series, follow her on social media, and more all at this link: https://linktr.ee/blyedonovan.